A Queen and A Hustla 2

Tina J & Karma Monae

Text Shan to 22828 to stay up to date with new releases, sneak peeks, contest, and more...
Check your spam if you don't receive an email thanking you for signing up.

Text SPROMANCE to 22828 to stay up to date on new releases, plus get information on contest, sneak peeks, and more!

Table of Contents

Previously...

Tish

I know you guys have heard nothing but bad shit about me, but let me make it clear that half the shit they said isn't true. So let me give you a quick rundown… My mom had two kids, who consisted of me, and I'd rather not disclose the other stuck-up bitch's name. Anyway, she gave my sister to her father while I was stuck at home dealing with mental and physical abuse by her. I'm not sure what happened to my mother or why she gave my sister to her father, but once she did that, everything was my fault, and she made sure to tell me that shit every day.

I met Farriq when I was working at JC Penny, as a Sales

Associate, and from the moment I laid eyes on him, I knew he was the one for me. We started off as friends, but things moved fast, and before I knew it, I had quit my job and was living in a huge mansion in Mount Laurel. I wish I could say something bad about Farriq, but honestly, I couldn't. He was the most perfect man I had ever met and all the love that I lacked from my family, he showed to me ten times more.

When Farriq's father passed the family business down to him, that's when things took a turn for the worse. His late nights turned into early mornings, and once again, I was back to feeling neglected and lonely like I had been when we first met. Youusef, and I crossed paths when I was taking groceries into my house, and I gave him head to say thank you. He and his brother, Yas, were infamous in New Jersey; everyone wanted to be affiliated with them, and it just so happened that, when Sef saw me, he wanted me… or so I thought.

Sef spoiled me rotten, only he did it behind closed doors, just like Farriq had before he became so caught up in the streets. I can't lie; it felt good to feel important for once. Yes, he had told me from jump that we could never be anything, because he was married and loved his wife, but if he loved that bitch so much, why was he always begging me to smash? I never intended to fall for his ass so hard, but I did, and when I loved, I loved hard, which was probably why I wasn't able to fully let go. With Farriq being so busy, I probably could have gotten away with creeping with Sef for so long, but as fate would have it, I got caught red-handed one day after spending the night out with Sef.

From there, our relationship deteriorated, and we were never able to bounce back from it. Did I regret fucking Sef? Hell no. That nigga had some bomb ass dick and knew how to do things to my body Farriq never did. What I did regret, was hurting Farriq to the point of no return. That's why I was happy as hell when I found out the bitch he had been dealing with was the enemy.

****

I got a phone call from Rashad telling me to get to the hospital, because Farriq had been shot. Before I could ask where he was, he banged on my ass. I really couldn't stand him; he always hated on me, and I had a pretty good feeling he was the one who snitched on me to Farriq about creeping years ago. So just how he didn't like me, I couldn't stand his ass either!

I walked into the emergency room and walked straight to the information desk. I had called every emergency room in Monmouth County since Rashad at least told me that much.

"Hi, my baby's father was brought in for a gunshot wound."

"What's his name?"

"Farriq Coy, Jr." I answered. It seemed like forever before the nurse started typing into the computer.

Finally, she looked up at me and said, "He's still in surgery. Have a seat in the waiting room and a doctor will be with you shortly." she said. Following the signs, I made my way through the crowded hospital to the waiting room.

"Tisha?" I heard a familiar voice call out.

"Hello, Chiya."

I turned and met eyes with the other person I didn't want to see, Chiya. I hated this bitch with a passion. She was sitting on a stretcher that was in the hallway, having her leg patched up by a nurse. Even with her red and puffy eyes, I couldn't deny, she was just as beautiful as the last time I had seen her.

"Wait, wait, wait... how the fuck yall know each other?" the little Spanish looking chick was walking up behind me. I noticed that she was one of the two bitches who jumped me in my house a while ago; I would never forget her face even if I tried. It made sense now; she was Sef's wife. She looked back to Chi who was trying to figure out what I was doing here.

"Farriq was shot-"

"Farriq?" They both asked confused as hell. That's when I realized, the Spanish chick didn't know who I was. She hadn't a clue.

"How the fuck do you know Farriq, Tisha?" Chiya

asked rolling her eyes.

"How the fuck do you know this bitch Chi?" The Spanish chick asked her again.

The three of us stood there looking at one another, waiting for the answer to the million-dollar question. A smile spread across my face and then Chi said, "She's…that's my sister."

Chapter 1

Yajari

"I never usually speak when I have my kill in front of me, but because you're my brother, I will. I did everything you ever asked me without questioning you. I dealt with all the different side chicks and ho's and never once did I question who those bitches were and if they had a motive. I make one mistake and fall in love with the enemy, who I didn't even know he was until you told me. An enemy that was beefing with my family over some shit between our fathers. You disrespected me, tried to choke me, and your brother shot my child's father." My mother covered her mouth and my dad slowly made his way behind me.

"So what? You mad he may not make it, or did he die already?" He smirked when my dad had his hand on mine.

Here I am pointing a gun at him, and he was still being the

cocky asshole that he is.

"Nah, he didn't die but you're about to."

"Oh my God, Jari, why would you shoot your brother?"

My mom yelled out and ran over to him. She put his head in her

lap and ran her hand over his forehead.

"Are you serious right now, Ma? I literally explained

what he did as far as putting his hands on me, and you're

questioning why?"

"Jari, let's go." My dad was pulling me out the hospital.

"No. I have to check on Farriq; well FJ." I saw the look

of hate in my dad's eyes, but it was too late for regrets now. I'm

a grown ass woman, and they're going to have to get over it.

"Get your ass in the car NOW!" He said in a tone that

made me do what he said. I could see the doctors running to

where Yas was. I noticed Chiya down on the ground lying there

too. I gave zero fucks about her right now. No one told her to

jump in front of my brother. He didn't care what he did to my

13

man, and I felt the same way. Yes, F.J. and I may have broken up, but the way he disregarded everything my brothers said and was willing to die for me made me realize that he was where I wanted to be.

I stared out the window replaying in my mind everything that took place in the last few hours. The man I was in love with was public enemy number one. My brother shot him, and I shot one of my brothers. My dad was deep in his thoughts because the entire ride to their house was quiet. He pulled into the driveway, answered his phone, and stayed in the car. I went inside and headed straight to my room that I used when I stayed here, then got in the shower. I looked down and FJ's blood was going down the drain or at least I thought it was. It was at that moment that I remembered that I was pregnant. I reached down in between my legs to check, and luckily, there was no blood. I was never able to see the doctor with everything going on, but you can believe I will make it my business to.

I finished handling my hygiene and threw some clothes

on with a pair of sneakers. I picked the clothes up and took them downstairs to put them in a trash bag and throw them away. My father was sitting at the island with a knife cutting an apple but staring a hole in my face. I walked past and ignored him, but if you know my father, he doesn't tolerate that; he felt it was a form of disrespect so I knew he was about to try and talk shit.

"Are you going to tell me everything that happened or am I going to have to beat your ass to get it out of you?" I looked at him like he had lost his fucking mind. I don't care how big my father was; him putting his hands on me at my age was not happening.

"Dad look. I didn't know who Farriq, FJ, or whatever y'all call him was, and he was unaware of my status too. Unfortunately, his nosy ass friend dug deep into my background and figured it out, then informed him. He asked me to kill my brothers as a test, and I told him no. I also let him know that, if he came for them, I was taking him out myself." My father nodded his head.

I went on to tell him everything that had happened in the meeting and how Sef wouldn't allow him to take me to the hospital after Yas choked me and dropped me to the ground. When I told him Sef shot him in the back, I wanted to spit in his face.

"No disrespect dad, but what do you mean that's your boy."

"Just like I said, Jari. That's my boy."

"Hold up. You're ok with your son making a bitch move and shooting a man in the back instead of the front like a real man would?"

"You're saying your brother isn't a man?"

"You damn right I am. You're sitting here in my face telling me you don't care that he was holding me to get me to a hospital, and that shooting him was ok. What if he would've missed? Huh? Or what if the bullet would've gone straight through and killed me?"

"But it didn't and now you're here crying over some fuck nigga." I wiped my eyes and glanced up at my dad who sat there without a care in the world. He went to get a water bottle from the refrigerator, and I moved to stand in front of him with my arms folded. He pushed me out the way a tad bit too hard if you ask me.

"I guess this must be put your hands on Jari day. First, Yas and now my own father. The same man who instilled in my brothers to treat me like a Queen and to never disrespect or lay hands on me. You think because you're my father it's ok?" I was now yelling.

"Let me tell you something. Yes, I taught my sons to treat you like that, but right now, you're being a spoiled bitch. You want me to take your side and tell your brothers that what they did was wrong. Grow the fuck up, Jari. There is a war out in these streets now that all this shit happened. People are going to find out who you are, and the threats are going to come on a daily basis."

17

"I don't care about any threats. You know I can handle myself."

"Handle yourself, huh? Do you know I had to call the Chief of Police and promise to pay him almost half a million dollars to make the hotel and hospital incident go away? I have to figure out what type of drastic measures I'm going to need to take to keep my family safe, and you know why?" He was towering over me, but I still stood my ground and stayed there.

"Because when that nigga's father finds out that one of my boys shot his, he will stop at nothing to get them. Yea, he may be in jail, but his reach is just as long as mine. So I'm standing here in this kitchen right now asking you, when the time comes to go to war, because trust me it's coming, where will I find you since you're so in love?" I stood there stuck because I didn't know what I was going to do. Yes, I loved my family, but I loved Farriq too.

"Your silence gave me my answer? Just remember this though. You think he ran back to his ex after he found out who

18

you were. What do you think he's going to do when he comes out and realizes a war has started? Do you think he's going to stand side by side with you? Or better yet, will that nigga give you the protection we've given you all these years?"

"Wait a minute? How do you know he ran back to his ex? Did you know he and I were together?"

"I'm your father, and whether you believe it or not, I have your best interests at heart. I've known about you and him since your first interaction at the club when you sprained your ankle. I always have people watching you even when you think I don't."

"How could you act like it was new to you?"

"I didn't know it was that serious until your brother told me about the pregnancy in the hospital." Just like Yas' punk ass to run and tell my parents everything.

"I can't believe you knew and didn't say anything. You talk about you were protecting me when the entire time that man could've switched up and killed me. The many times he came to my house, when he whisked me away for vacation, and even when he was at my house with your favorite granddaughter. Anything could've happened, and you knew this whole time."

"You're being dramatic now."

"Dramatic." I scoffed up a laugh. This man had me all the way fucked up.

"You call me dramatic, but this entire time, your beef has trickled down to your kids, which almost got all of us killed. We have been beefing with a guy for unknown reasons, and all you can say is I'm being dramatic. You're fucked up, Dad, and I'm making sure I tell Mom how you put us in harm's way."

"You don't have to tell me anything. I already know." My mom said coming in the door.

"Mom, please tell me you didn't know about Farriq too."

"I knew, but I don't have to tell you shit just like your father doesn't." I stepped back to look at my mom because she's never spoken to me in a disrespectful way either. Today seemed like everyone was shitting on me for something that I was blind too.

"You were sleeping with a man whose father is the archenemy of yours. You may not have known, but you would've known that had you not tried to keep him a secret. The day you met him, it was your responsibility to inform us so that we could check him out. You know that, Jari, but you wanted to be grown, and now you're caught in the middle of it." I put my head down as I now listened to my mom go in on me.

"I'm a grown woman, and maybe I'm tired of getting approval from my parents and my siblings. All my life, I was told I couldn't have friends because of what I was being groomed to be. Then, you had to pick my boyfriends. The house I live in, the car I drove, the killings I did was all because of you. I haven't done anything on my own, and I think it's time I started living for me and not everyone else."

WHAP!

I felt my mom's hand go across my face, but my reflexes kicked in and I went to hit her back. I would never disrespect my parents, but what she did was uncalled for, and I reacted quickly. I felt my body being lifted and tossed against the wall as my father held me up by my shirt.

"If you ever in your life raise your hand to your mother again, I will beat the shit out of you. Do you understand me?" I didn't say anything. I had nothing but hate in my eyes at the moment.

"Jari, did you hear what the fuck I said?" I felt his hand around my neck, but he wasn't squeezing. I nodded my head. He let me down hard, and I tried to catch myself but fell.

"You should've let her hit me Omar so she could see how I would've whooped that ass." I didn't say anything as I listened to her talk shit. I took my phone out my pocket and went to the Uber app to have them send me a driver. I picked up my keys and purse and headed for the door.

"Both of you know that I'm with child, yet you put your

22

hands on me as if it doesn't matter."

"Girl, don't nobody give two shits about that bastard baby. If you know what's good for you, you better terminate it." I felt the tears stinging my eyes, but I've been doing so well holding them in since earlier I wasn't about to let my parents see them fall.

"That's how you feel about my baby." My mother rolled her eyes, and my dad flat out said yes.

"Let me say that I never in a million years would've thought that my own parents would treat me like shit. To have you both put your hands on me and then call my baby, your grandbaby, a bastard showed me that I no longer want to be a part of this family. When I leave this house, I am leaving all of you... your drama, disrespect, and hatred towards my child, behind me. You won't ever hear from me again."

"Jari, if you walk out of here, you are no longer my daughter. I will disown you and all your enemies will be that, yours. You no longer have a house, you will leave the cars, and

your bank account will be closed the second that door closes."
My father said coming towards me. My mother stood there with
her arms crossed sucking her teeth.

"It's ok, Father. I need to find my own way, and I can't
with you, the woman who birthed me, or my siblings hating
me." I heard a horn blow and opened the door.

"Jari." My father yelled out as I started towards the Uber
driver.

"I heard you loud and clear."

"Jari, I'm warning you." I turned around, and that's
when I saw my mother letting the tears roll down her face. The
entire time she talked shit, and now that I was going to stand on
my own two feet, she felt bad. After she hit me and talked shit, I
didn't feel one ounce of remorse for either of them.

"I won't bother you anymore since I'm such a burden,
but know this." I saw the both of them standing there waiting
for me to speak.

"All I wanted to do was have a family and raise them the

way you did with my brothers and me. To show this baby that our family was built on love, and that we were strong, but right now, at this very moment, the only family my child will have is its dad and I." I opened the door to the car that was waiting for me.

"Oh, if you come for my man or me, I will kill you. If you send someone to make me lose this baby if I already haven't, I will kill you." I could see the shocked look on their faces. "Go tend to your sons; I'm sure they need you. Goodbye Omar and Zora Abdul."

I closed the door to the Uber and laid my head back on the seat crying my eyes out. The driver kept asking if I was ok. I didn't know what I was going to do with no money, no house, no car, and no family. All I knew was that my child and I were going to be alright, and that's all that mattered.

Chapter 2

Farriq

I heard the machines beeping as I tried to open my eyes. When I did, the sunlight was blinding me, and my throat felt like it had something inside of it. I pulled on it, but the more I pulled, the more it felt like it would never stop coming out. When it finally did, I tossed it to the floor and snatched the tube from under my nose, then did the same thing.

I removed the blood pressure cuff and started to disconnect the heart monitors. The machines were going crazy, yet no nurses came running in. *What kind of hospital is this?* I thought that, when the machines went haywire, they would. I tried to stand, and that's when I remembered I was shot. The pain was excruciating, and my legs felt like noodles as I moved them to the edge. I felt the cold air on my back from my gown being open, so I put my hand in the back to close it and felt the bandages that were there.

"How are you doing today, Mr. Coy?" I heard and turned around. There was a doctor and nurse standing there lusting over me. I admit they were both fine, but damn, a nigga was in the hospital. I felt exposed and couldn't help but laugh at how they saw me in an uncompromising position.

"I'm good considering. How long have I been here?"

"Two weeks sir." The doctor answered and helped me lie back in the bed so she could exam me. She placed the light in my eyes and checked my throat, which she informed me was red and inflamed from me snatching the tube out. The nurse handed me some water as the doctor finished checking me. She went to lift the gown up from my waist, and I smacked her hand down.

"I apologize, Mr. Coy. I need to check you."

"That's all good, but my dick wasn't affected, and you trying to sneak a peek. Have you been doing it the entire time?" She started blushing. I sucked my teeth, because she was unprofessional as fuck. She had me lift up so that she and the nurse could change the bandages on my back.

"Sir, you are healing pretty well. Do you remember what happened?"

"Yup, and no I don't know who did it." I spoke firmly and gave her a look not to ask me any more questions about it.

"Well, ok then. Everything seems to be fine. You are a very lucky guy."

"Yea, yea. Just tell me when I can get the fuck out of here." I wasn't beating around the bush with her thirsty ass.

"Well, if everything goes well, you can be out of here by the weekend."

"What's today?" I asked unaware of the day.

"Monday."

"Monday. Hell, I'm not waiting that much longer to leave. You're bugging." I was about to say something else when I heard a voice I knew all too well.

"My son is right. He is not staying until the weekend. You can have his discharge papers drawn up for him now." I looked up, and it was Stocky. He was my dad's right-hand man. He was like Rashad and me; when you saw one, you saw the other. The doctor and nurse both left, and Stocky closed the door behind them.

"What up, Pop?" I asked trying to get comfortable in the bed. He was on Facetime, and the look on his face was telling me he was about to go in.

"You tell me. What's this I hear you were sleeping with The Silent Assassin, got her pregnant, and is it true that it was her brother that shot you?" I could've lied, but if my father was asking, it meant he already knew. I confirmed what he said and listened to him go off about how the streets are talking and the war has just begun. They were waiting for both of her brothers to get out the hospital.

"What you mean get out the hospital? What happened to them?"

"When that nigga Youssef shot you, Rashad shot him. After Omar and his family heard what happened, they all went to the hospital, and his daughter came in and shot the other son, Yassin, and his girlfriend." I was pissed when he said that, because I told her not to act on impulse. I know she was mad at both of them, but they were still her brothers.

"Son, I'm about to ask you a question, and I need you to answer it honestly." I blew my breath and waited for him to ask.

"Why didn't you kill her when you found out who she was? You know the type of beef we have with them."

"To be honest, Pop I was already in love with her. I had my gun to her head, but I couldn't do it. The crazy part is, she told me she didn't try and set me up, but I didn't believe her until the day I got shot. We were sitting in that meeting, and she was shocked to see me. When her brothers told her who I was, she was surprised and mad at me for not telling her."

"Is that your baby?"

"Yea." I smiled a little at the thought of her carrying my seed. I wanted her to have my kids, but I didn't think it would be so soon.

"She will be under our protection now, because her family disowned her; well, she disowned them. They have sent two people to kill her already, and she has taken them both out. Now that she is pregnant with my grandbaby, I will make sure no one touches her."

"What type of family is she dealing with? Who does that?"

"Son, when you're feeling better, I need for you to make a trip to see me. There's a lot of things that you don't know, and I think it's time I told you."

"Roll call." I heard someone yell in the background.

"Stocky is going to take you to my house, and I want you staying there until shit blows over. If it doesn't, then that will be your new home." He hung up, and Stocky put the phone in his pocket and handed me a bag of clothes. I would have to take a shower at home, because I needed to get out of here and find Yajari. I was struggling to put my boxers on lying in the bed when I heard some heels coming in the room.

"Baby, when did you get up?" Yajari screamed when she saw me. She came to me and kissed my lips, then turned her face up.

"What?"

"Baby, your breath stinks. Come on, and let me clean you up." She called Stocky in to help her take me in the bathroom. There was a seat and retractable showerhead in the shower, so she was able to wash me without getting my back too wet. She helped me put my clothes on and paged the nurse to come change my dressings before we left.

"You look sexy as hell." She was wearing some tight, black jeans with a fitted, white V-neck, and some red bottom shoes. Her hair was down, and she wore no makeup. My girl was gorgeous, and I wasn't about to allow any man or woman to take her away.

"Why thank you?" She smiled and kissed me using her tongue this time. I felt my dick getting hard and moved her back when the nurse cleared her throat. She changed my dressing and sent the doctor in, who had a scowl on her face when she saw Yajari. I was happy my girl was looking down on her phone, because she was no joke with them hands, and I would hate to have to kill the doctor for getting beat up and pressing charges.

The doctor went over the care instructions I had to follow when I got home and told Yajari that my back should be changed three times a day for the next week. She also told me that I had to follow up with a doctor to get my stitches out a few weeks after that. The nurse had me sit in the wheelchair and took the ride downstairs in the elevator with us. I noticed Yajari staring at the nurse as she tried to make small talk, and so did Stocky, because he was smirking.

"Ok, Mr. Coy. You're all set. Good luck."

"Hi, Nurse Tasha." Yajari said glancing at her name tag. The nurse folded her arms like she was about that life.

"I know my man is fine as hell, and I'm sure you checked his dick out a few times when he was out of it, but let me tell you one thing. That's me all day, and the next time I see you being that thirsty up in his face, we are going to have a problem."

"Hold up, bitch." She had her finger in my girl's face.

"Fuck." I yelled out. I could barely move and Stocky went to get the car. If anyone knew Yajari they knew she hated to be called that. I watched my girl yank the nurse up and throw her against the wall. She pulled the gun out her waist and rammed it in her mouth.

"If you ever in your pitiful life fix your mouth to call me a bitch again, I will blow your motherfucking brains out. You got the right fucking one."

"Yajari." Stocky yelled and pulled her away from the nurse, who was crying hysterically. It wasn't a lot of people in the lobby, but the few who were, were pointing but no one said a word. Thank goodness I didn't see anyone with a camera phone, because it would've been hell trying to get the video. I loved the fuck out of my girl, but she was certified crazy.

****

"Yajari. I'm sorry for not believing you and allowing Rashad and Tish to get in my ear." I said to her as we were on our way to my place to get some things before we went to my father's house out in Cherry Hill.

"Why did you run to her?"

"I didn't run to her. When you left, I was pissed and drunk an entire bottle of Henney. She knocked on the door, and for some reason, I thought it was you. She claimed to have come to see my son. I left her downstairs and told Ellie to go get the baby out his room while I jumped in the shower. I didn't have any business driving, but I was coming to see you. I had my clothes on and was on my way out the door when she came barging in knocking me off balance. Being that I was almost drunk, she was able to get my pants down and put me in her mouth. I should've stopped her, but I was weak. When I saw the look on your face, I was fucked up. I never cheated on you and always told you I would never hurt you." I could hear her sniffling as she stared out the window.

"I understand."

"Huh."

"I should've told you who I was from the beginning, but I didn't think it was necessary. You thought I set you up. I don't condone what you did because of it, but I understand. Farriq, when I told you I loved you more than any other man, I meant that. A lot of shit happened when you got shot. I lost my family, and I now have people trying to kill me courtesy of my father."

"Your father." She nodded her head.

"Where have you been staying?"

"In different hotels. My father had all my accounts closed, but thanks to my sister-in-law Rosa, she's been renting me rooms under her name. Farriq, I don't care about that materialistic shit. The only thing I was worried about was you and my baby." She rubbed her stomach with a grin on her face.

"Look at me." I lifted her chin.

"You are still my woman, and I am going to take care of you."

"Farriq?"

"Yajari, cut it out. You are staying with me, and you are under the protection of my pops and me. No one will be able to get at you. I know your father has a long reach, but mine does as well." I pecked her lips and kissed her tears away. I stared at her and couldn't help but smile. There was nothing I wouldn't do for her or my kids.

We stopped by my house and picked up Ellie and my son. I wasn't back to walking perfectly yet, but I was ok. I heard the doorbell ring, and I assumed Yajari went to answer it.

"What the fuck are you doing here?" I could hear Tish all the way from upstairs, yelling. I stood by my door and watched my girl handle it.

"What do you mean what am I doing here? For one, this is my man's house. Yes, you heard me, my man. Two, whatever you thought you had with him is over. He had a weak moment and let you suck his dick, but I can guarantee you will never make him cum the way I do." I had to grab my dick when she said that. Yajari definitely did things to me sexually that no other woman has. She had me strung-out on her pussy.

"You ain't all that with your broke ass. The whole hood and state of New Jersey knows your family disowned you and left you out to dry. From what I hear, they're trying to remove you from this earth. You can occupy this spot for a minute, but once you get caught and take that dirt bath, trust, I'll be back."

"I see you have no idea who you're fucking with. Bitch, I am your worst nightmare. I'm the woman your momma and daddy warned you about." She pulled that gun out and placed it on her temple. I really had to take that shit from her. She took that thing out every chance she got. Tish looked like she was about to shit on herself.

"I will exterminate you right here in front of your son and baby daddy without thinking twice. You have one more time to come at me, and I will erase any remnants of you from this world and have your son calling me mommy. You have been nothing but a pain in the ass for me and my sister-in-law. When are you going to get it through your head that none of these men want you? You are a fuck to them, and that's all you'll ever be. Niggas don't make hoes the wife; remember that." She chucked up the deuces, pushed her out, and slammed the door in her face.

"You make my dick hard." I told her moving slow down the steps.

"I'm sorry I said the part about making your son call me mommy. I would never try to take her place." I pulled her body into mine.

"If she doesn't get it together, that's exactly what's going to happen anyway. Now, come on. You're going to love my father's house.

Chapter 3

Youseff

I had been lying here in this bed staring at the ceiling for the last twenty minutes trying to figure out what the fuck happened. It had been two and a half months since everything went down. One minute, we were having a meeting, and the next, I wake up in this rehabilitation facility with doctors explaining to me that I was temporarily paralyzed from the waist down. Each day, they had me up doing therapy, and the minute I thought I could feel my legs, they would poke me with something and I wouldn't feel anything.

Throughout everything, my wife, my rock, and my heartbeat was there through it all. I asked her every day why she was there, and her answer remained the same. It was always that she loved me, and there was nothing anyone could do or say to keep her away. I told myself that I was never going to hurt her again. In my situation, it's always good fucking with new pussy but old pussy was the only type to hold you down. Rosa showed me daily that she would always be down for a nigga, and I appreciated that and her to the fullest.

"Hey, Daddy." My daughter came into the room and jumped on the bed to give me a hug. It was her first time seeing me since the shooting. I didn't want her to come up here at all, but Rosa said all she did was cry and beg, so I allowed her to come.

"Hey, Baby Girl. I missed you." I hugged and kissed her all over her face.

"Ok, Mr. Abdul. It's time for your therapy session." The older man said. Rosa told them when I first got there no woman would be working with me.

"Daddy, can I go?" I looked at the therapist, and he

nodded his head yes. He guided my legs off the bed and lifted me to the chair. I felt like a handicapped person, and I didn't like it. We got in the room, and the guy pushed my chair to the front of the walking beam after exercising my legs first. I stood up and held onto the rail. He moved my legs down at the bottom, and I took one step and almost fell.

"It's ok, Daddy. I fall all the time on the playground." I stared at my daughter and somehow had the urge to keep going. I needed to get all my strength back to run around with her again. I noticed Rosa on her phone texting back and forth, but ignored it for the moment.

"That's good, Mr. Abdul. Do you feel yourself moving?" He asked me.

"No."

"Well, you're moving on your own." Rosa popped her head up, and I saw tears come down her face. She put everything on the bench and came closer to where I was. I wasn't walking fast or anything, but I took maybe five or six steps. My daughter was jumping up and down clapping.

"Ok, Mr. Abdul, I think that's enough for the day. You don't want to continue and strain yourself. If you're taking this many steps today, just imagine how many you'll take tomorrow." He helped me back in my chair and pushed me to the room. After I had got back in the bed and my daughter put the headphones on that she got for her birthday, I decided to ask Rosa who she was talking to.

"I'm talking to Jari." I cringed my face up. It wasn't that I didn't love my sister, but the reason I'm in here is partly because she was with some dude we were beefing with. I know she didn't know but so what.

"Don't do that, Sef. You know as well as I do that you two miss each other."

"Whatever." I waved my hand at her.

"Baby, tell me what happened that night?" Rosa never once asked me what happened, and I was curious as to why she was now. I thought back to the meeting.

"She'll be fine, Farriq. Put her down."

"I don't care about this meeting. I didn't even want to come. My boy is more than capable of handling this situation. Right now, I have to get my girl, your sis... I mean, assistant, to the hospital." I noticed how he didn't blow her spot up and expose her. I lowered my gun when all of a sudden I heard some noises come from behind me. I turned around and saw this nigga with his gun pointed, and FJ had blood coming out the back of his shirt.

"What the fuck nigga? He has my sister, who is pregnant, in his arms. Why would you shoot him? Matter of fact, I don't even care. Get the fuck out." I turned around and felt two burning sensations. I knew then I was hit and fell on the floor.

"I'm taking this shit from you and your family." He said and walked out the door. I felt myself losing consciousness by the second. Yas came in calling out for me, but I couldn't move. I rattled the chair the best I could, and thank goodness he was

paying attention.

"Sef. Are you ok?" Rosa yelled out bringing me back from that dreadful day.

"I'm good, baby. I don't want to talk about that right now." I told her and kissed her forehead, then her lips. She and my daughter spent the day with me. We talked, played, and even ate dinner that Rosa had delivered from the pizzeria. I couldn't wait to get home and do this all the time.

****

A month later, I was released from the rehab place. Every day after I took those few steps, it seemed like I was taking more and more. I wasn't speed walking, but I could get around on my own with a cane. Rosa hired a therapist that came twice a week to help me regain full use of my legs.

With each day passing, I got better and better. My parents invited us over for dinner, and Yas wasn't too happy about it. We knew it would be some shit being this would be the first time the issue was brought up again. After dinner, my wife and daughter assisted my mom in the kitchen to clean up while we went to my dad's office.

"I'm going to need one of y'all stupid motherfuckers to explain how your sister ended with that fuck nigga?" We both looked at each other and shook our heads.

"Ok. Since you can't answer that, Yas you can tell me how you didn't know that little hoe you're sleeping with was a stripper?" Yas jumped up ready to defend her, but the minute pops gave him that look, he took a seat.

"Let's be clear about something. You two niggas are supposed to be kingpins... the fucking BOSS, yet all this bullshit is going on. Yas, you're supposed to check out every bitch you fuck with thoroughly. How did you miss that? And Sef, you didn't think to check out that side bitch you had either? Huh? If you had, you would've known who her son's father was. How can you call yourselves anything when you're slipping for some pussy?"

"I guess Jari is exempt from all this." Yas said.

"FUCK THAT SPOILED BITCH! SHE IS NO LONGER MY DAUGHTER!"

"Wait a minute, Pops. Don't disrespect her like that." He came over to me and stood in my face. I was pissed I had this cane but I'd swing that shit quick if I had to. Pops or not, he could get it.

"Your sister went against the grain for some dick."

"Pops, you know she didn't know." I was trying to get him to see it from her point of view.

"I don't give a fuck. She should've checked his ass out too. Then, she comes up in here talking about she choosing her man over her family." My eyes widened when he said that. There was no way my sister would choose a man over us. Definitely not me. Whether I'm talking to her or not, she and I were close.

"She said that?" Yas asked, and we were both shocked when my dad nodded his head.

"Y'all better start checking everybody out from now on.

I don't care if it's a play date for my granddaughter. Her entire family needs a background check. And you, Yas, need to get rid of that bitch Chiya. Your mom told me she's sisters with the bitch Sef was sleeping with. I don't trust either of them." After all the yelling he did, I slowly walked out the office and had my wife and daughter meet me in the car.

"Ma, tell me it's not true." I said when I pulled away from the hug.

"What baby?"

"Did Jari say fuck us so she could be with that man?" She rolled her eyes and walked back in the kitchen. "Ma?"

"What Youssef? Your sister is selfish and she chose the life she is living now. I hope it doesn't cost her, her life."

"HOLD THE FUCK UP! I KNOW DAMN WELL THERE WAS NO HIT PUT OUT ON HER!"

"Boy, who do you think you're talking to?" My pops came in.

"Look, no disrespect, but I'm telling you right now, if I

find out there was a hit put out on my sister and who arranged it, I'm killing everyone involved. I don't care who it is." Both of them stood there quiet. Yas searched my face to see if I was serious, and when he noticed I was, he shook his head and left. Did this nigga know something I didn't? I grabbed my cane and left as quickly as I could. I don't know what the fuck was going on, but the minute I found out, bodies would be dropping. At the end of the day, that's my fucking sister, and no one was going to take her life. No one.

Chapter 4

Courtney

The moment that fucking gate closed to the prison gate, I dropped to my knees and wanted to kiss the ground. However, that shit wasn't happening being as though dirt would be all over my mouth. I put the bag on my shoulder and walked to the bus stop. I could've had someone pick me up like my mother, but I cut everyone the fuck off once I got in here; especially, my snitch ass brother. I still remember that day six years ago like it was yesterday.

"Court, I'm going out of town for a week, but when you're ready to pick up, call your brother. He will bring everything to you." FJ *said and gave me a hug. That was my brother from another mother. He and I were tighter than me and my own brother Rashad.*

"Ok. Be safe and let me know when you get there." He kissed my forehead and left my apartment to go to the airport. I locked up and threw some clothes on to go work out at the gym. No matter what I was doing, I always made it my business to stay in shape.

Two days later, it was time for me to pick up the product and distribute it to all the trap houses and the DMV area. The connect Rico would send us to take it there if things were hot down there. In return, they would occasionally do the same thing.

Anyway, Rashad met me at the warehouse, handed me everything I needed, and took off. The entire time, he was acting nervous, which was odd, because that nigga wasn't scared of anything or anyone, except for FJ and the connect. I'm not sure why he was scared of FJ, but he was downright petrified of him.

Me and another one of the soldiers named Arthur packed everything in the truck and got in. Arthur was my dude that I trusted wholeheartedly and vice versa. He and my best friend were engaged to be married, and I was the matron of honor. The wedding was a few weeks away, and he was nervous.

"Boy, cut it out. You know damn well that woman loves you."

"I know, right. But what if I can't be the man she needs?"

"Arthur, cut it out. After five years, if you weren't, she wouldn't have said yes." He nodded his head and lit a blunt. After a few pulls, he passed it to me and pulled off. We got to the first trap, unloaded, and left. We did this for about five of the ten traps we had before we noticed a black car following us.

"Yo, hit up all the traps in a group message and tell them 187." He said. 187 meant the cops were lurking and to dead all sales and put everything up in the vaults that were built in the ground. If the cops searched, they wouldn't find anything and dogs couldn't sniff shit out because it was padded.

"What the hell is this about? FJ has the cops on payroll. Whoever this is must not know who we are." I said, sending Farriq and Rashad a text message.

"You know what, you're right. Change of plans. Resend a message to the traps saying 911." That message stood for getting the product and money out the house.

"If someone is following us, that means it's a snake in the camp." He was right. Each house only had two workers in it when we dropped off, so if anything were missing, we would know who the snitch was. Each person at the trap had a secret hiding spot for cases like this. The only person who knew where they were was FJ; my brother didn't even know. FJ was very smart and would always tell us that no one person needed to know all your secrets and some things should be taken to the grave. The lights went on, and that was it.

"Get out of the car." The officer said and both of us complied with no back talk. The cops had Arthur and I handcuffed, standing on the side of the police car. They went to

the back of the truck, lifted up the rug, then the tire, and pulled

up the secret compartment. They found the drugs and the guns

and arrested us on the spot. Needless to say, I tried to take all

the weight so that my best friend could marry the love of her

life, but neither one of them were trying to hear it. She told me it

was part of the game, and she understood. The wedding could

wait for both of us.

We both got six years for distribution, intent to

distribute, possession of a substance in a school zone, and

possession of illegal firearms. The lawyer FJ had worked on

our case was the shit and well worth the money. They tried to

give us twenty-five years to life for the amount of shit we had. It

was crazy, and I found out Arthur and I were released on the

same day. I called my best friend to tell her and she was crying

and telling me she couldn't wait for both of us to get there.

Unfortunately, I had to tell her the bad news that I

wasn't coming back to Trenton right away. She informed me

that all my money I had her get from my house before the cops raided it was in the bank collecting interest under her name so

they wouldn't touch it. She had me on the account and told me

to get a temporary ATM card from the bank when I got out. I

promised her I would come see her the minute the dust settled,

and I meant it.

I took a bus up North and ended up getting a room at the Holiday Inn Hotel in Totowa, NJ, which was close to Paterson. After I checked in, I took a hot bath, threw on my wife beater, some black skinny jeans, and a pair of Jordan's I picked up from the mall that wasn't too far away. I grabbed my room key and the keys to the rental car I had and went out looking for a bar to have some drinks. It had been a long ass time since I had the taste of an ice-cold Corona going down my throat.

I wound up at some club that FJ's friend Mook owned. I only knew because he ran down on me the second I walked in. He told the waitress all the drinks were on the house. I ordered a Corona and drank that shit so fast the bartender ended up giving me another one before I asked. Mook and I kicked it for a while, but he had to go handle business. He told me I could stay with him and didn't take no for an answer. He gave me the address, his house key and told me he would see me later. No, we never had sex or anything. I was that cool chick that all the niggas loved.

"Yo, aren't you that nigga Rashad's sister from the down South Jersey area?" Some dude asked me.

"Yup." I sipped my rum and coke drink I had just ordered. I didn't care that I was mixing drinks. It was my first day home, and I was enjoying it.

"We don't take kindly to snitching ass niggas or their family members up this way."

I looked at him sizing him up before I spoke.

"Well, I guess we have something in common because that snitching ass nigga is going to get exactly what he deserves when I catch his ass." I could tell I caught him off guard by the way he stroked his beard looking at me. He sat next to me, and we started talking, and truth be told, dude was cool as hell. We exchanged numbers to hang out another time. I didn't plan on hanging with him, but I would definitely use it to my advantage.

The club started picking up and the hoes were in full effect. Half-dressed, naked women and nothing but men that you could tell were balling. I noticed one dude walk in that was sexy as fuck. I could tell he was somebody by the way bitches were flocking to him like bees to honey. His dreads were pulled back in a rubber band and his clothes were definitely expensive. I couldn't tell you what his shoes were, because I'd been in jail so long I had to catch up on the style. His smile caught me off guard, because not only did he have all his teeth, but the dimple that crept on the side of his face was mesmerizing.

"Don't stare too hard; I may think you want to take me home." He chuckled and found a spot next to me. The bartender automatically brought him a drink without asking what he wanted. I assumed he was a regular here.

"That may be right, but you're not ready for a woman of my caliber."

"What's that supposed to mean?" He sipped on his drink eye fucking the hell out of me.

"It means I'm not looking for a man, but I'm trying to fuck. I'm talking about no strings attached, and you would only see me to make me cum." His smile got wide.

"Seems like you met the right nigga. I'm not looking for a chick, and I just need to get my dick wet. What's up?" I laughed at his bluntness.

"You tell me. This is where I'm staying tonight. If this is what you think you can handle, then allow me to ride that ride."

"Really, Yas. You're all up in this bitch's face while I'm at home waiting for you." I wasn't going to say anything until she called me out my name.

Yas…so that's his name.

"Honey, this ain't what you want. If that's your man, whatever problem you have, take it up with him, but don't come to me on no rah-rah shit. I will lay you the fuck out, take your dude home, and fuck the shit out of him." I saw the chick's entire demeanor change.

"Yas, you're going to allow her to speak to me like that?"

"First off, Chiya, this woman has done nothing to you. You brought your rowdy ass in here talking shit to her for no reason. Take your ass home." I saw him yank her up and push her out the door. The bitch had ruined my mood, and I was ready to go.

I sent Mook a text telling him I would be there tomorrow to stay. I stepped out the club, and she was yelling in his face as he stood in front of a Phantom. Our eyes locked, and I licked my lips and blew him a kiss. She turned around and tried to step to me.

"Look Miss whatever your name is. You were right, I shouldn't have stepped to you like that in the bar, because you didn't know he was my man, but now that you know, you're being real disrespectful, and I'm trying not to fuck you up out here." She had her arms folded with a pout on her face. This bitch really didn't know me, and I hated to be the one to have to school her.

"That's cute."

"What's cute?" Shorty shot back at me.

"You." I spat. "You're out here acting like you're tough. I like pretty bitches like you who run ya mouth like you can fight. You probably lick a mean pussy too." I said flicking her hair and laughing. " Let me break it down for you sweetie. I will fuck your life up out here and not give two shits about it. If that's your man, tend to him and stop worrying about me. The next time you call yourself stepping to me make sure you have someone by your side to pick your ass up off the ground once I knock you out."

"You're not knocking shit out bitch." That was twice she said that, and I had warned her. I hit her ass so hard she went flying back into the car. Her so-called man stood there laughing at her. Once she gained her balance back, she tried to charge me again, but I pulled my gun out and put it straight to her forehead.

"Again. This ain't what you want. Go home little girl. The next time I won't be so nice." She backed up and ran to her car crying.

"I'm following you or what?" The nigga said. He wasn't shit, but he isn't my man.

The second we got to the hotel, and I closed the door, we were all over each other like animals in heat. It was probably the alcohol for him, but for me, it was the lack of sex. He lifted my wife beater off and unsnapped my bra while I removed the belt and unbuckled his jeans. Once I removed all his clothes, I was impressed like a motherfucker. Now, usually I wouldn't suck a man's dick, but his was calling out for me, and I had to fulfill my needs. I took him in my mouth whole, and prayed that I remembered what to do. With all the new shit out that chicks did with their mouths I read in books, I wanted to make sure I didn't look stupid.

"Shit, Courtney. Suck it just like that." He moaned out and grabbed my hair. I didn't recall telling him my name but right now wasn't the time to focus on it either. He gently guided my head back and forth. I glanced up at him, and he was smiling down at me biting his lip. I used my hands to jerk him off and sucked on his balls one at a time.

"Oh shit, girl. I'm about to cum. Stand up." I appreciated the fact that he didn't want to nut in my mouth but I wanted him to. I made my mouth like a vacuum and sucked harder until I felt him stiffen up and release everything he had. I stood up and removed the rest of my clothing, then sat on the bed. I expected this nigga to be ready to fuck, but he got on his knees and took me to places I have never been. His head game had me screaming, banging my fists on the bed, gripping the sheets, and trying to run.

"Fuck Yas. I can't take anymore. Please."

"Cum for me one more time." I tried not to give it to him because he had already gotten three out of me and I felt like he was being cocky, but it was no use.

"Ahhhh shitttttt, Yas." I screamed out and felt like I was pushing a baby out. My pussy was gushing out liquid, and he drank it down to the very last drop. I laid there breathing heavily as he kissed up my body. He sucked on my stomach, then my breasts. He found his way to my neck, and I could tell he was leaving hickeys. We were now face to face with one another, and it was like everything stopped. I wasn't a kisser, and I think he felt the same, but at this moment, it was calling me. I took a chance and wrapped my hands around his neck and slid my tongue inside where he happily accepted it.

"Damn, Courtney, I don't think I'm about to allow you to fuck anyone else. This pussy right here is worth all my money." He said stroking the hell out of my g-spot. My legs were over his shoulder shaking like a leaf. His pounded in and out kissing me in the process.

"Ride this dick and let me see if you're worthy for me to make you my wife." I laughed at his crazy ass. He was so cocky and arrogant, and I loved that shit.

I got on top and slid down slowly to get used to it. The euphoric feeling it gave me had tears falling down my eyes. This nigga had me gone with his dick game, and I didn't know how I was going to allow him to go back to that chicken head.

"What's good, Ma? Why the tears?"

"It's been a long time, and this dick is good as hell." He sat up with me still riding him. His hands went up and down my back as he sucked on my chest. I leaned back a little and continued riding him until we both exploded. I laid down on his chest. He removed the hair out my face and wrapped his arms around me. I don't know when, but I fell out not too long after. He literally put my ass to sleep.

Chapter 5

Yas

I had to leave my parents' house when I heard Sef say he was taking out whoever put a hit out on my sister. I strongly doubt that my father did it, but the way he called Jari out her name, I can't be so sure now. After Yari shot me, a nigga was beyond mad, but when I sat back and thought about it, I understood. I was her brother and her protector. I did some fuck shit by disrespecting and putting my hands on her. I may not fuck with her like that, but I'll be damned if anyone goes after her.

I went home and got dressed to hit the club, because I wasn't trying to sit up under Chiya. Ever since her ass got shot, she's been talking real grimy about my sister. I know she was upset and didn't know who Jari was, but who told her to jump in front of the bullet. Granted, she showed me she was down for me, but the minute she mentioned trying to get back at Jari, my feelings were changing.

I stepped in the club, and there stood a female I hadn't seen in years. Yes, I knew who she was, but I never approached her, only because she was the sister of an enemy. Unfortunately, I heard what went down and how her brother was the one who supposedly ratted her out. If she was out here, that meant she was up to something.

She was definitely a bad bitch. She had to be at least five foot seven with a nice ass, decent size titties, and her swag was not the same as most chicks. She put me in the mind frame of a hood Keri Hilson. You know, that gorgeous type but would still shoot your ass. Her hair flowed down her back, but what caught

67

me were the tattoos that were on her arms. I could see some on her back from the wife beater she wore. And let's not talk about those thick ass child-bearing hips she had.

The shit kicked off with her and Chiya, and shorty rocked the shit out of Chi. I laughed, not only because it was funny, but because Chi thought she could beat every female out there. Shit got real when the gun came out. I swear Chiya shitted on herself by the way her face turned up and she ran. I followed ole girl to the hotel, and we fucked the shit out of each other. Now, Chiya had some good ass pussy, but this chick right here had poison between her legs, and I'm not talking about that bad shit. I'm talking about that type to have you killing niggas over it and having me not even wanting to look at another woman.

After she had fallen asleep on top of me, I slid her over so I could use the bathroom. I got a warm rag with soap on it and washed both of us up. She stirred a little in her sleep but not enough to wake up. I stared at her pussy and found myself eating it again. Chiya was the only woman I kissed or went down on, but for some reason, this woman right here screaming out my name made me want to give her all of me. We had each other moaning, and by the time we were finished, it was daylight, and we were knocked out in a spooning position.

"Where are you going?" I asked, when I opened my eyes and noticed her putting clothes on. Courtney was in a cotton robe, with a scarf wrapped around her head and slippers on. This was her room, but she was laying clothes out on the bed about to leave. She had a nigga feeling cheap as hell right now.

"Ugh, I'm about to leave…" she said, with a confused look on her face. "Look, I just came home from jail, and I needed some dick. I must say, I'm happy you were the one I got it from, but there's money to be made and moves to be making, Lil' Daddy. I'm bout to raise up," I sat up on my elbows and looked at her.

"Come here." I waited for her to stand in front of me. She hesitated for a minute, and I could tell she wasn't used to following orders.

"First off, I know who you are, and where you came from Lil' Mama, so you ain't gotta school me for shit. Second, you're not going anywhere until we get some sleep and go out to breakfast. What I look like letting my girl leave out tired and hungry?"

"Your girl?" she asked, with her eyebrows raised. I shot her a sly smile and gripped her by her wide hips.

"Did I say that? I meant to say my future girl. I have some loose ends to tie up, but you will be my girl shorty."

"What the fuck ever?" She said, and I started pulling off her robe and guiding her to get back in the bed. My phone was going off nonstop and it had been all night. I guess Courtney was tired of it, because she snapped, reaching over and answering it.

"WHAT bitch? If he's not answering, it's because he's busy! Damn!" She yelled into the phone. I heard Chiya on the other end telling her to put me on the phone, while I removed her panties and had her sit on top of me. My dick was hard as hell, and hearing Courtney lay down the law had me ready to fuck her insides up. She reminded me so much of myself that it was crazy.

"He's busy right now." I heard Chiya desperate ass ask her what was I doing.

"I'm about to ride his big ass dick and let him fuck me into a coma again. I promise to send him home before dinner." She laughed after she hung up.

"Well. What are you waiting for?" I asked her as she kissed my lips.

"What you mean?"

"You told her you were about to ride this big ass dick. Get to it." I said smacking her ass. We had sex, but this time, neither of us moved afterwards and we fell straight to sleep. I woke up, and it was five in the afternoon. Courtney was knocked out. I had ten missed calls from Sef and about twenty from Chiya along with some text messages. I called my phone from hers to make sure we had each other's number and left. When I got to my house, I saw fire trucks and cops. *What the fuck did this bitch do?"*

****

There were at least four ambulances and a dozen police cars, and it seemed as if all of my neighbors were surrounding my crib. I lived in a nice, gated community with condos, and I had the entire first and second story condo for myself; it was built as if it were a house. Judging by the looks of it, it was still intact. There was smoke debris all over, and I just knew that that stupid bitch Chiya had something to do with it. I saw Sef standing there talking to the police, and he pointed my direction as I walked up on them.

"What the fuck happened?" I barked. Sef shook his head at me like he was saying something without saying it.

"Mr. Abdul, I'm Detective Rollins. We received a 911 call about a fire from one of your neighbors. It seems as if your bathroom in the master bedroom had been set on fire. We were able to stop the fire, and it didn't spread to the rest of the house, however, the second floor of your home is completely damaged. You won't be able to stay here tonight sir." My jaw tightened, and I was ready to fuck some shit up for real.

"Was there anyone else home?" I asked.

"No sir. However we received a statement from an eyewitness who said there was a woman who fled the scene." He handed me his card. "In a few days, you can get a copy of the police report. Sorry for your inconvenience." The detective walked off towards the other officers, and I stood there holding the card with his name on it in a daze.

"I told you not to trust that bitch after she pulled that stripper stunt." Said Sef.

"Mannn, shut the fuck up! Stupid ass bitch ran down on me at the bar last night while I was kicking it with this shorty."

"A shorty?"

A smile crept on my face, thinking about Courtney's fine ass. I hated that I had to leave her, but I knew that, if I didn't leave, she would have me busting her shit down all day. She had that wanna-layup pussy. The type of shit that makes a nigga not even wanna run the streets.

"Yeah, brah, I met this chick last night. Hold on real quick," I stopped talking and answered my phone; it was my pops calling. Something told me he knew what was going on.

"What up, Pops?"

"I told you to cut that hoe off, didn't I?"

"Pop-"

"Cut that stripping ass bitch the fuck off NOW!" he screamed hanging up in my ear.

I shook my head stuffing my phone back in my Versace pants. It seemed as if the fire trucks and ambulances were starting to leave one by one and the neighbors had retreated to their own houses. Me and Sef walked and let ourselves inside my crib to look at all the damage. The moment we stepped in, my finger literally itched to blow this bitch's head off.

The entire ceiling was smoke-stained, and half of it was caved in. I was standing in the fucking kitchen looking up into what was supposed to be my bedroom! There was water damage all over ruining my furniture and shit. All of my clothes were ruined, and I had no upper half to my house.

"Dammmmmm, bruh… this bitch Lisa Left Eye'd you." I shot Sef a look, and he threw his hands up and did the Fergusson stance.

"Hey, I ain't do it, don't shoot me." he joked again.

"Yeah, you right. I'll holla at you, bro. I'm finna go see this bitch." I said, heading back out the door.

"Wait, what about here? What you gonna do? You need me to tell Rosa to make up the guest room for you?"

"Nah, I'm good. Just do me a favor and get someone to have my cars from the garage brought to your crib. I'll holla at you later yo."

****

I hopped in my truck and did ninety all the way to Newark, New Jersey. Chiya knew I was going to come looking for her ass, so her best bet was to get out of dodge. I knew she wouldn't leave without getting her shit, though, and she thought I didn't know she had kept her little apartment.

Even though I had never technically asked Chiya to move in, she had most of her shit there, but I knew her type; she wasn't about to give all that up. She was too independent. I pulled up on South Orange Ave and 15th street to where her apartment was.

Her car was right out front, and it looked like she was loading her shit up just like I had thought. When I let myself in, she was coming right down the steps carrying a large china bag filled with clothes. Our eyes locked, and she dropped the bag taking off back up the steps but tripped over her own feet stumbling right back down. I grabbed her up by her neck and looked in her tear-filled eyes.

"Come here, bitch!"

"Yasss!!! Stoppppp!!" she cried.

"You like setting my shit on fucking fire, Chiya!"

She was gagging by the pressure I applied to her neck. I wasn't trying to kill her; I just wanted her to see the light a little. I was so angry I didn't see the sneaky bitch lift up her leg to kick me in my dick, making me fall flat on my face, while grabbing my nuts.

"Ahhh, fuckk!!!" Chiya lay beside me scrambling to her feet.

"How you gonna come up in here beating on me after you stuck your dick in that ugly, black ass bitch! How could you do that to me, Yassin?"

"You set my house on fire, Chi! For real though? I don't give a fuck about what you talking about; I lost everything!!!!" I barked. We were both on our feet and in a standoff. I was ready to beat her ass now.

"You promised me you wouldn't hurt me, Yas! You promised! I gave you my heart, and you shitted on me for some fat bitch who looks like she was on cell block D!"

I didn't mean to laugh, but I did. Chi kept referring to Courtney as ugly and black, but she was neither, and Chi had eyes, so she knew that too. Courtney was beautiful as hell. What stood out about most was her natural beauty. She didn't wear no 'inches' as these bitches would say, or that fake lashes shit. I hated all that extra shit. One of my pet peeves was when a bitch's lashes hung off on the edges looking like bird feathers and shit.

Courtney ain't have none of that going on. Her long hair hit the middle of her back and was long and silky, just like my mama's. She had smooth, mocha skin, and thick, long lashes that went perfectly with her full, pink lips. I was truly infatuated with her, and hearing Chi talk cash money shit reminded me why I ended up cheating in the first place.

"See… you can't even deny it, can you!" Chi screamed, breaking me out my thoughts.

"What the fuck you want me to say Chi?"

"The TRUTH!!!"

"You want the fucking truth, Chiya? Okay, here it is. Yeah, I cheated. I fucked her, and I stayed at her spot all night while she took this dick and sucked me like a porn star. And I loved every minute of the shit. That's why I didn't come home last night. That's what you wanna hear, huh, Chi? You want me to tell you how I let another bitch console me and make me forget about all the fucked up shit I've been going through these last two months?" For a brief moment, we both just stood there staring at each other. Chiya let tears roll freely down her cheeks, and I could see the heartache written all over her face. The fucked up part about it was I didn't feel an ounce of remorse for what I said either.

"Why? How could you do this to me? I-I-I was there for you, Yas. I took care of you-"

"Nah, you reminded me! Every day, you made it your business to kick Jari's back in about what she did to me and how you wanted to get her back. You thought I ain't know you been plotting on her Chi? You know damn well she related to me, and not once did you even stop to think about how her being hurt or killed would affect me and my family. But I'm supposed to love you?" I snapped. Chi stepped back looking offended.

"She fucking shot you, Yas! She shot me!"

"So! No one told your captain save-a-hoe ass to jump in front of the bullet for me! I told you I would handle the shit. You running around here worried about her, but when is the last time you paid me any attention? When is the last time you sucked my dick Chi!"

"So-so. This is because I don't suck your dick now?" she said.

I sucked my teeth and ran my hands down my face. This bitch was making me so mad I didn't even want to talk to her ass anymore. The fact was I cheated, she burned my crib down, and we were done.

"You don't get it, Ma. This is because we ain't right for each other. I got a lot of shit going on right now. I'll admit I was wrong for cheating, but it is what it is. The fact is, you burned my shit down, and too much has happened to come back from, so fuck it." I said shrugging my shoulders. I reached into my pocket and pulled out a big knot of cash, then handed it to her. It was the least I could do for her going through all my bullshit. The way I saw it, I could get another crib, but you can't get another life. I wanted to live my life every day like it was my last. Chi just wasn't the one for me to do it with.

"So you think you can hand me money and walk out, and that's it? So fuck me, Yas, huh? You don't even know how I feel! Who said I couldn't forgive you?"
Now that shocked me. Chi had never come across as desperate, and right now, she was sounding like it.

I cocked my head to the side, "Come on, Ma. You're better than that. If you were to rock with a nigga after fucking around on you I wouldn't even respect you the same and you know that. Before I walked up in here, you was halfway ready to haul ass. It ain't working, Chi. I'm not happy no more, and you ain't either. Take the money and move on with your life."

I gave her one last look and headed for the door. I had shit to do, and the last thing I was trying to do was argue with her ass all night about a dead issue. I really did care about her, and I didn't want to hurt her, but I also knew I wasn't through with Courtney yet.

Halfway to the door, I hear Chi yell out, "Yas, wait… I'm pregnant!"

I paused mid-stride, back still turned, and said, "Kill it."

Once I made it out the door, I hopped back in my truck and hopped on the parkway to head back to the hotel. Chi saying she was pregnant really fucked me up because there was a strong possibility that she was. As much as it hurt me to tell her to kill my child, I knew it would be for the best. I couldn't see myself with Chiya, and the last thing I was trying to do was be tied down to someone I didn't see myself with for the rest of my life. At twenty-six, I didn't have any kids, and I'll be damned if the one I had would be by someone I didn't wanna be with. Fuck that.

Chapter 6

Tish

"Fuck!" I screamed, throwing my phone at the wall and breaking it into pieces.

I had been calling Farriq's phone for days now, and he had yet to answer any of my fucking calls, thanks to that little bitch of his. Every time I called, it would go to voicemail, and I was sure her ass had everything to do with it. It had been like this ever since he had gotten shot.

Getting up from my living room couch, I walked to the kitchen to light a Newport off the stove when my house phone rang. After taking a long drag, I looked at the caller ID hoping it was Farriq. It was Chiya.

"What?" I snapped, not even knowing how this stuck-up bitch had gotten my number. Before seeing her at the hospital, I

84

hadn't seen her in years. I wonder why the bitch was calling me now?

"Ugh-Tisha, um… are you busy?"

"Yes, what you want?"

Chiya cleared her throat before she spoke again, "I-uh.. I need a place to stay. Me and my boyfriend aren't seeing eye to eye right now, and my lease is up on my apartment. I have to move out by tomorrow or the constable is going to lock me out."

A smirk rose on my face; this prissy bitch needed help from my ass, now, huh? After all these years of her ass acting like she was too good for the hood, I was shocked she would be willing to come live in the jungle. I guess shit was really fucked up on her end.

"Chiya, girl I got bills, and I can't be taking in no strays-"

"I can give you two thousand today." She blurted out.

Sold. This dumb bitch gave me 2,000 dollars to stay up in the projects where I was only paying $82 a month for rent. Now, I wasn't any fool, so I damn sure accepted and told her to be on her way. A bitch was so happy I even helped her carry her shit in. Since my son lived with his father full-time, I decided to let Chiya use his room until she found her own spot, whenever that would be. My son would just have to sleep with me when he came over; it wasn't like his father let him stay over that much anyway.

"Tish, you got any tampons?" Chiya asked, walking in my bedroom.

I was up watching some reruns of *Martin*, after my long ass shower I had taken. In a few more minutes, I was going to be knocked out, but this dumb bitch came interrupting me and shit.

"Yeah, it's under the bathroom sink."

"Thank you."

"Mmhhm," I said, waving her off.

Since I was fully up again, I got out the bed and headed to the kitchen to get a glass of water. Chiya was in the bathroom handling her business, and I could hear her on the phone going off like a mad woman.

"So you're really done with me, Yas! After I tell you I'm carrying your fucking child, you just abandon me for that ugly ass bitch! Niggga Fuck You!!!" Now, I was no doctor, but how was this bitch pregnant when she had literally just asked me for some tampons? I stood off to the side of the sink drinking some water, when the bathroom door opened, and Chiya stepped out with bloodshot red eyes.

"Pregnant, huh?" I said, wearing a smirk. Chiya rolled her eyes and sat at the kitchen table dropping her head into her palms.

"I don't know what to do." She cried. "Yas is done with me. I burnt his house down after he was creeping with some bitch named Courtney. I can't believe he would play me for that ex-con." My antennas went up at the mention of Rashad's sister

Big Court. She was infamous in the hood, and we all knew there wasn't shit ugly about her ass either.

" Are you talking about Big Court?" I asked, taking a seat across from her at the table.

Chiya shrugged. "I guess. Stupid ass bitch got to talking out her face at the bar last night, and I stepped to her." With my eyebrows arched, I urged her to continue.

I knew about Courtney first-hand after being around Farriq, and I knew damn well, if Chiya stepped to her, Court laid her down. She was known for fucking up bitches and having shootouts with niggas. I ain't know her personally, because she had gotten locked up way before I met Farriq, but I knew she was Rashad's sister and had the dope game on smash prior to her getting locked up.

"I didn't even know she came home."

"So you know the bitch too?" Chiya spat. She was jealous as hell, and it was showing like a mothafucka.

"I don't really know her, but I know of her. She used to run with Farriq and Rashad before she got cuffed. Rashad is her younger brother. I heard they offered her ass twenty-five-to-life, but Farriq paid some top-notch lawyer to get her ten. Word around the way is Rashad snitched on her, but I doubt he did; Rashad is not like that."

"Sounds like you're really close to this Rashad guy."

"Something like that." I said, not wanting to touch on the subject.

"So what's up with you and your dude? Why he kick your ass out like a bad habit." I joked. Chiya didn't find me amusing but she answered anyway.

"He cheated on me, and I burnt his house down." I was sitting there waiting for her to say sike, nah, or just playing but it never came.

"Are you really pregnant?"

"What you think!"

"Whoaa… calm down boo. I was just asking the tea honey. No need to get all hostile cause ya man kicked your ass out. Shit." I said, lighting up a Newport.

"I'm sorry, girl… I just can't believe, Yas- " My mind went to going when she said that name. I had heard it from somewhere before, but I couldn't place a face to it.

"Yas? As in Sef's brother from North Jersey? The Abdul Brother's?" Chiya nodded her head.

"Yeah, you know them? I know Rosa and you had a few words at the hospital; what was up with that?" she asked.

"Oh, that bitch was just still salty behind me fucking her nigga Sef for the last year. I guess she found out, and they broke up. The little bitch and her sister came over here and called themselves jumping me and shit." I said, waving her off. The shit was something light to me, because I planned on seeing them bitches.

"Oh… you must be talking about their 'relative' *Yajari*." I couldn't help but laugh at Chiya. Her ass was jealous as hell of any other female that wasn't her. Me? I could give two fucks.

I started laughing, "Relative? You believe that shit huh? Girl, that's their sister; don't let them fool you. That bitch came over here with Sef's wife going off about her brother. They not low. Now Farriq running around her behind her stinking ass. I wouldn't be surprised if he got shot behind that hoe." Chiya shifted a little in her seat, and I could sense she was a little uncomfortable. "What?"

"She. She the one that shot me and Yas at the hospital that day." I started choking on my cigarette smoke after I accidentally swallowed the smoke.

"Bitch, what? Wait, so let me get this straight. Yajari shoots you and Yas, then Yas cheats on you with the enemy's sister? What type of shit yall got going on?" I couldn't help but laugh.

"Well, from what I heard, the family not fucking with her after she got pregnant with Farriq's baby. Apparently, she didn't know Farriq was FJ, and Mr. Abdul done put a hit out for the bitch and everything." My stomach tightened, and I started to feel queasy.

"F-Farriq got her pregnant?" I asked again.

With a slight grin, Chiya said, "Yup."

Chapter 7

Yajari

The hit my parents put out on me caught me by surprise.

I didn't think me branching out on my own would piss them off.

The day I left my parents' house I checked in at a hotel and paid

for a month with the credit card I had before I was cut off. That

night, I had just gotten out the shower and heard the door chime

letting me know someone entered the room. Imagine my

surprise when I saw one of my dad's most trusted bodyguards

with his gun pointed at me. The crazy part is, it was pointed at

my stomach. I knew then they had no intentions of killing me,

just my child.

"Really, Eric? You're going to kill my child for a man that would have me take your entire family out without thinking twice?" He smiled and lowered his weapon before walking close to me. I saw the way he licked his lips and knew where this was going. I dropped my towel and allowed him to follow me to the room. I scooted back on the bed and watched as he unbuckled his pants and let his boxers drop with them.

"Do you know how many years I've watched your sexy ass? I know this pussy is going to be worth it." He climbed on the bed, and the second he tried to lie on top of me, I removed the gun from under my pillow and shot him right between the eyes. I jumped up and dialed hotel security and told them someone came into my room trying to rape me and that I needed the cops there. This was my alibi, and I was sticking to it. My gun was registered, so I wasn't worried.

Once the cops left, I told them I wasn't staying in the hotel any longer and went to my car. I hit the alarm, grabbed the door, and felt something pushed in my back. I turned around and saw Eric's partner. I kicked him in the balls, grabbed his gun from him, and shot him a few times in the head. Lucky for me, he had a silencer on his so I was able to get away with it. I left him there and drove until I almost fell asleep at the wheel. Thank goodness Rosa called me that night to check on me; I ended up staying with her for a few days. I didn't stay longer than three days, but she knew my parents had cut me off and paid for my hotel stay until Farriq got out. He tried giving her the money back, but she wouldn't take it.

I closed the door after I watched Rosa and my niece pull away from Farriq's father's house that we had been occupying since he was released a few months ago. I still had no contact with my parents or siblings. The only one I saw was Rosa and my niece who wanted to stay with me but couldn't. Sef was already suspicious of where Rosa went, because she never told him. If my niece would've stayed, I could see him coming down here to get her, and there's no telling what would happen.

I walked upstairs to take a hot bath and relax. I was now five months pregnant; my stomach was big but not huge. I was probably the happiest I had been in a very long time. The hot water I stepped in was just the right temperature to make my body loosen up and enjoy myself.

"Right there, baby." I moaned out with my eyes clothes. Farriq always came in the bathroom unannounced. If I was sleep, him massaging my clit and having me on the break of cumming was always the way he woke me up.

"You better not cum yet."

"Why not?" I started whining, because my pearl was extremely hard, and I was right there.

"Because I want all that in my mouth." He stood me up and sat on the edge of the tub, lifted my leg up, and finished me off with his mouth. Farriq may have a great dick game, but his head game was enough for me to tap out and not need the dick. He had me step down out the tub as he still sat there. He slid me down on top of him and moved my hips in a circular motion on top of him the way he likes it.

"Damn, Jari. I'm never letting you go. Fuck! This pussy is by far the best in the world." He bit down on my shoulder and sucked on my neck. A few minutes later, we both released. He moved my mouth to his and kissed me with an intense passion that had both of us hot again.

"How was your day baby?" I asked him once we washed up after our sex session.

"It's always a good day knowing I'm coming home to you." Farriq wasn't doing as much as he was before he got shot, but he did leave out during the day to check on his traps and do business with his shady ass friend Rashad. I'm a good person to read people, and that nigga has been sheisty from the very beginning. Something about him rubs me the wrong way, and I can bet he's planning to do some crazy shit.

I tried to speak with Farriq about it, but he swore that Rashad would never cross him like that. I left it alone, but you can bet I was keeping my eyes and ears open.

"Isn't that sweet? You're just saying that because you just had your daily meal."

"You can say that too. That will always cheer me up." He stood behind me and kissed my neck while I put on my nightclothes. He rubbed my stomach and whispered in my ear.

"Jari, I didn't plan on getting you pregnant, but I'm happy that you're having my baby. I wouldn't want anyone else to be my child's mother. I love everything about you from the inside and out. Our child is not going to be brought up the way we were and will know we love him or her." We didn't want to know the sex of the baby yet.

I knew he was talking about us growing up in the street life and the way my family was treating me. The crazy part about the shit with my family is I didn't care that we weren't on good terms. I mean, yes, I miss talking to them. Especially, my brothers, but I feel at peace. I don't have to kill anyone, and as far as I know, I have no enemies down here so I wasn't looking over my shoulder. If I did have them, Farriq's father had so many bodyguards on me, like I was Michelle Obama they would never get close enough anyway. I had two in the black bulletproof Suburban with me at all times, even when I went in the store. There were always two more Suburbans behind us with more guards, and he even had people watch the cooks if Farriq and I went out to eat. I told them it was a bit much but they were not budging.

****

Today I made plans to go to Babies"R"Us to shop for a crib and the other big items. I wanted Farriq to come but he had a meeting with the connect Rico and he had a feeling it wasn't going to go well. I tried to go with him but he wasn't hearing it. He wasn't sure if my brothers would be there, and he didn't want to kill one of them for hurting me. I know I said I would kill him first if he came for my family, but at this point, he was protecting me and his child. I couldn't dare ask him not to.

"Hey Stock, what's up?" I asked Farriq's father's right-hand-man. I was scanning all types of shit in the store.

"I heard you were here. What is that in your hand, and why do you look like you're shooting items?" I laughed because he had no idea. Farriq probably would've asked the same questions had he been here. I explained what I was doing and found it quite amusing that he stayed in the store with me. I wasn't sure if he had kids, but by the looks of things, he was ecstatic that I was pregnant. After I finished and picked up some diapers and wipes that he carried out for me, he helped me into the truck. He nodded his head at the two guards and we drove off.

"Where are you taking me?" I asked when I noticed us going in a different direction than my house. I went to reach for my phone to contact Farriq, but my purse was missing. I know damn well these niggas weren't trying to kidnap me. I glanced outside the truck and felt a little better seeing that Stock's car was in front of us. We pulled up to some huge house that appeared to be owned by white people just from the neighborhood we were in.

"What's going on Stock? I know damn well Farriq isn't going to be happy when he realizes I'm not there." I asked when he assisted me out the truck.

"Don't worry about him. He'll be fine. I have someone here that wants to speak to you." I stopped walking towards the house and stared at him.

"If it's any of my family members I don't want to see them." I turned to walk away.

"Listen, Yajari. These last few months you've become like my long lost niece and I would never allow anything to happen to you. As far as your family goes, you should know me better than to think I would let any of them around you. My nephew loves you, and not only would he and his father kill me if anything happened to you, I would never forgive myself if it did. You can trust me." I saw the sincerity in his eyes and gave

him a hug. He was right. Over the last few months, he has been

like the uncle I never had and made it known that he would

never allow anyone to harm me. I wasn't used to going

anywhere without Farriq knowing so I was a tad bit nervous.

This pregnancy had me vulnerable, and I didn't like it one bit.

Stock opened the door to the house and the inside was

decorated out of this world. I saw African-like sculptures and

other ancient-looking artifacts. The television was on in the

front room, and I could smell some food cooking. Stock called

out to someone and a woman walked out. She was an older

woman, and if I wasn't mistaken, her ass resembled Farriq more

than I cared to admit. She was about five foot five with a

chocolate skin complexion. Her hair was cut short like Halle

Berry's used to be, and her body was amazing to be a woman of

her age, which looked to be no older than forty. She stepped

closer to where I was and put both of her hands on my face. I

moved back and she smiled.

"You are as beautiful as everyone said you were." She sat down on the couch and patted the seat next to her. I opted out from sitting that close and plopped down in the recliner. Stock shook his head laughing, and I heard what sounded like a back door open and shut. Some man walked in, and if I thought Farriq resembled this woman, the man who came in could've been his twin.

"Somebody better tell me what the fuck is going on. You can start by explaining to me why both of you resemble my man." I folded my arms and stared at both of them. I didn't have any weapons on me, but I wasn't going to play some quiet bitch either.

"First off, let me say I apologize for bringing you here without your knowledge. Second, my son wasn't lying when he said any man that saw you would be mesmerized by you. Yajari, you are beautiful." The man said. I blushed a little bit but rolled my eyes.

"It's ok, honey. I would be standoffish as well if I had

two people speaking to me and yet to know who they were. I am Tammy, Farriq's mother and-"

"Wait a minute. You're supposed to be."

"Dead. I know." She stayed finishing my sentence.

"That's a long story, but this is Farriq senior, and before you say it, yes he is supposed to be in jail. Fortunately for him, he has been home for a week now."

"Does your son know all this? I mean, how is all this even possible?"

"Hey baby." I turned around, and Farriq was coming through the front door.

"Did you know they were bringing me here? What is going on?" He lifted me up and kissed my lips.

"Yes I did. Ma, did you feed her yet?" He asked her and ignored what I said.

"I didn't get a chance to because she wasn't trying to move from that spot until all her questions were answered."

"Come feed my baby, Jari. I know you're hungry." He

grabbed my hand and took me into the kitchen. I sat down at the island while his mom made me a plate that had my stomach growling extremely loud making everyone laugh. She made some greens, ham, potato salad, baked macaroni and cheese and cornbread. My mouth was drooling as I watched her fill my plate up. No one was allowed to eat before me, which I found hilarious.

"Oh my goodness, these greens are delicious. I haven't had this in a long time. My mom would make them for me once a month." I guess everyone noticed how sad I got because the room got quiet. I know I said it didn't bother me that I didn't fuck with my family, but being here with his brought back memories.

"It's ok, sweetie. You've been through a lot, but that's still your family."

"That's not my family. My family wouldn't be trying to kill my child or me. Do you know the first man who made the attempt on my life pointed the gun at my stomach and not me?

The other guy waited for me by my car. How could my father do that to me? That's ok, because he never has to worry about me or my baby." I slammed my fork down and excused myself from the table. I opened the back door and went over to one of the benches out there and sat down.

"You good, Ma." Farriq sat next to me. I put my head on his shoulder and he wiped my eyes.

"Yea. I just had a moment."

"Son, go see what your father wants. Let me talk to Yajari alone." He kissed me and disappeared into the house.

"Yajari, I know it must be hard for you knowing the things your family has done to you, but you have to understand that they are very upset with you, not because you did anything wrong, but because you defied them and continued a relationship with my son. Then, the entire fiasco that occurred in the hospital wasn't an easy pill for them to swallow either. Honey, by no means am I saying you're wrong, but this is a family that has kept you in the dark about things from their past that they don't want to get out." I looked over at her and asked her to elaborate on what she was saying.

"In due time that information will be told to you. Right now, let's get you back inside to feed my grandbaby."

"But-"

"But nothing. Let's go." She helped me up and turned to me. "Yajari, you are carrying my grandchild, and the minute my son announced his feelings for you, there was no way you would ever be put in harm's way. The word is out, and your parents are furious that you have his father's protection." I noticed how she said his father's protection. *I know I'm missing something here but I don't know what.*

"I do need you to realize a time will come that you will have to choose sides. I'm not saying you have to do it right now, and we would never ask you to go against your family, but the time is coming and your family will be waiting." With that being said, we reentered the house, and there were more people than before, which I found out were more relatives.

Farriq had me sit next to him in the kitchen while he spoke with his dad about who knows what. I devoured that food and asked his mom to make me a plate to go so everyone wouldn't eat up everything. Farriq took my plate and put it in the sink.

"Oh my God, Farriq. I've missed you so much." I turned around and some bitch jumped in his arms.

"Oh HELL FUCKING NO!" I shouted and everyone looked at me. I started walking to where they were.

"Aw shit." I heard Farriq say.

Chapter 8

Farriq

"Aw, shit." I said loud as hell not caring who heard me. When she jumped in my arms, I saw the look on Jari's face and knew shit was about to go left. I put her down and she kissed my cheek oblivious to my woman coming towards her. Stock jumped in front of Jari just in time as I moved the chick behind me.

"You got five seconds, nigga, to tell me who this is or we are going to have a problem." Yajari slipped her shoes off and already had her hair going up in a ponytail. She was crazy as hell over me so I didn't think this would end well at all.

"Who the fuck are you?" Courtney said and came from behind me.

"I'm his woman, and why the fuck you jumping in my man arms?" I could see the smirk on Courtney's face.

"Well, well, well Farriq, I see you got yourself a pit bull for a woman."

"Bitch, did you just call me a dog?" Jari was now standing in front of Stock, and I was trying to pull Courtney back since she walked around me.

"That's what you're acting like. You're coming at me like I'm some bitch off the street. You don't know me, and I can tell you this ain't what you want." Courtney said pissing me off.

"Oh honey, I think you better ask around about me. See, my name is Yajari Abdul." I saw Courtney's facial expression change. "Oh, I see you know the name, which means you know our background. Everything you heard is true and don't think for one second because I'm pregnant that I won't fuck you up."

"Farriq, you need to control your woman."

"Courtney, shut the fuck up and don't say shit else to her. You're lucky you family, because I was two seconds from fucking you up. You know I don't play that disrespectful shit

when it comes to who I'm with." She rolled her eyes.

"Now, Yajari, this is Rashad's sister, Courtney I told

you about, and Courtney, this is my woman Yajari."

"Hold up. You're sleeping with the enemy and no one

has come for you yet?"

"Who said she was the enemy?"

"FJ, I know that last name. Shit everyone does." I hated

when she called me my street name, and she knew it. I guess

this was her trying to get her point across.

"We can talk about that another time."

"I'm ready to go, Farriq. Ms. Tammy, I apologize for

disrespecting your house." Jari said. My mom gave her a hug

and told her not to be a stranger. I opened my car door and

helped her get in. I saw Courtney walking towards us and

blocked Jari's door. Her window was down so she could hear,

but there was no way Courtney would get any free hits on her.

"Farriq, we need to talk."

"That's fine. Talk."

"I don't want to talk out here. Can I come over?" I glanced at Jari.

"As long as you don't jump on my man or bring no bitches to my house, we good."

"Damn Farriq, she ain't playing no games with you."

"Hell no and vice versa. Courtney, I think she is the one." I told her when we walked to the back of the car.

"Really." Her eyes widened with excitement.

"Yea. As you can see, she plays no games about me, and she's about to have my baby."

"I'm happy for you, Farriq." She gave me a hug and said she would stop by later. After we walked in, Jari went upstairs to take a shower. She claimed it would calm her down, and right now, I needed her to be if the two of them planned on being in the same room.

"You good up here?" I asked when I noticed she wasn't downstairs after twenty minutes. She was pulling a shirt over her head. Her body was still beautiful to me even with her stomach.

"Yea. I'm coming."

"Yea, but you're not coming the way I want you to." I whispered in her ear as I stood behind her. My hands went inside the sweats she threw on and had her cumming on them minutes later. She turned around and wrapped her arms around my neck.

"You know better Farriq." I smiled because she was right. Anytime I made her cum with just my fingers, she had to have the dick right after. I made her get on all fours so I could get a quickie in.

"Throw that ass back for me baby. Yea, just like that. Fuck I'm cumming." I shot everything I had in her. The way she threw her ass made me cum fast, and I wasn't ashamed to admit it.

****

The next day, Jari wanted me to go with her shopping at the mall. I don't know what for, when she had enough clothes, shoes, and bags to last the next two years. Fortunately for me, I was able to get the new Jordan's that came out. I brought my son and the baby a pair to match mine. If we had a girl, I would bring them back and get her the pink ones. We did pick up some neutral things that she had to have.

Jari was on her way to the bathroom again for the hundredth time, but I wasn't complaining knowing it was my baby on her bladder.

"Why haven't you been answering my calls, Farriq?" I heard Tish say behind me. Some chick stood next to her eyeing me up and down. She wasn't bad looking but she wasn't shit, and I knew that from the way she licked her lips at me and licked around that ice cream cone like she was sucking a dick.

"Tish, why would I do that? I don't like you, and we don't have anything to speak about."

"Farriq, my son stays there."

114

"Bitch, what did I tell you about calling him that?" I had her backed against the wall. If one didn't know any better, it looked like I was trying to get close to her. Shit, Jari must've assumed the same thing because she went the fuck off when she saw me.

"Farriq, are you fucking serious right now? I think you're trying to make me kill your ass. Is that what the fuck you want?" She was standing behind me mad but looking sexy as hell.

"Jari, you know damn well ain't shit popping with this bitch."

"Farriq, you got her pregnant? How could you do that to me?"

"That's my woman and what I do with my dick and who I allow to carry my child is my business. Fuck out of here with that Tish."

"What the fuck does she want Farriq?"

"She wants to know why I haven't answered her calls

and claims she wants to see my son." I had my arms wrapped around her waist while she went in on Tish.

"Bitch, he hasn't answered your calls because when my pussy isn't in his mouth he's dicking me down. I want to thank you for fucking up, because I would've never been able to sample that good ass dick that you're over here trying to hop back on." I laughed and so did the guards that walked up when they saw Jari get upset.

"I know you want that old thang back, but honey, he's upgraded to the platinum pussy package."

"Fuck you bitch."

"Bitch. You need to be saying your prayers to God right now."

"For what?"

"Because if I wasn't pregnant, I would beat the fuck out of you and this stupid bitch you're with. Luckily, I have respect for my body and my baby, but trust and believe, I'm coming for you boo. And you too." She mushed both of them in the head.

"I wish the fuck you would, Tish." I said when she went to swing on Yajari.

"Oh, so she can fight me, but I can't fight her?"

"Yup. Pretty much. You already know what's going to happen if you lay one hand on her. I suggest you keep it pushing or be prepared to feel my wrath."

"Yea bitch. Take you and your pissy ass friend back to the projects. Remember what I told you while looking for the next come up. Ain't no nigga going to wife a ho, and if you're going to be his ho, play your position."

Jari had me stop at the store on the way home to pick up something for dinner. We got steak, mashed potatoes, corn, and a bunch of other shit we didn't need. I thought we were going for dinner and we ended up filling two carts. This woman was spoiled anywhere we went. After I brought all the bags in, and we put everything away, she started cooking.

"Thanks for dinner, baby." I kissed her lips and cleaned off the table. She told me she was taking a shower and that we were watching a movie together since I've been on the go. I felt bad not being there during the day, but she never complained and I loved that about her. I turned the light off in the kitchen and went to see what was on.

"I thought you told me your mom was deceased and your dad was in jail." I heard her say walking around the couch. She sat down next to me and waited for me to answer. I figured she would ask sooner or later, and it was no time like the present to tell her. I went to speak but the doorbell rang.

Chapter 9

Courtney

"What's up Court? You wanted to talk so spill it." Farriq

said when I closed the door and sat down in the living room.

Yajari was lying down on his lap while he rubbed her hair. I've

never seen Farriq this affectionate with a woman. He must

really love her to, not only have her at his house, but let her

carry his child. Farriq was a very private person when it came to

any of his relationships, so I was very surprised to see this side

of him openly. I took a seat on the couch opposite from them

both and gave Yajari a warm smile, even though the bitch had a

serious attitude problem.

"Hello."

"Hey," she said back to me just as dry as I was.

"She good right?"

"Bit-"

Yajari's words were cut short, by Farriq's voice.

"Man, Courtney, if she sitting here then that means she good, right? The fuck. Both of yall starting to get on my nerves with this shit. Jari, this is like my sister, and Court, Jari is going to be my wife. Both of yall chill the fuck out. Damn." Both Jari and I nodded and let him have that. We were being a little territorial, I could admit.

"So what's up Court?"

"I wanted to talk to you about your friend Rashad. I heard that nigga still fucking with you, and I find it crazy that you would even fuck with his rat ass after he got me cased up, so I figured the only reason he would still be on your team, is if either you didn't know, or you were sleep walking him. So which is it?"

I noticed Yajari sit up straight, removing her head from

Farriq's lap when I mentioned Rashad's name as if she had a personal interest. Farriq's eyebrows furrowed, and he massaged his chin.

"What the fuck you talking about Court?" I could see in his eyes, he had no clue what I was talking about.

For the next ten minutes, I sat there running down the chain of events that led up to my arrest. I also let him know my discovery had the name 'Big Court' on it, which only our crew referred to me as. I wasn't the only person who had gotten cased up and accused Rashad either. my nigga Paco from the north side was also arrested two days after me had said it too. Word around the way was that Rashad was a certified snitch, and it seemed as if everyone knew it except Farriq, or maybe he was that blind.

"Come on, Court. This shit doesn't make sense. Why would your own brother snitch on you, yo? Yall came out the same womb, bruh." Farriq said, after I was done putting it all out on the table. Yajari shot him a funny look when he said that,

121

and I was sure he didn't miss it either.

"I'm telling you, that nigga is a snake, and the only reason the Feds ain't pick your ass up was because I held those charges and cleared your name, but trust me, nigga, they knew all about our operation. Drops, pick-ups; they even knew about ya pops. Think about this shit, Farriq. You were out of town, and the only other person who knew about that drop was Rashad, and he was supposed to be there." My phone went off with a text from Yas, asking me where I was at, and I couldn't help but smile.

I hadn't known his ass too long, but he was mad cool and knew how to dick me down properly. As soon as I was done here, I planned on heading back to my hotel room so he could eat my pussy from the back to the front like he promised in his text.

"Court. I'm saying though. What motive would Rashad have for doing some shit like that? He was eating. Shit, this nigga run all the damn traps, my nigga."

"Sometimes you can feed a mothafucka ya whole plate and that shit still don't be enough." Yajari said. Farriq gave her a look, "You believe this shit too, Ma?"

She shrugged. "I'm saying… it's not surprising to me. I told you I didn't trust that nigga from the jump. I know a snake nigga when I see one, and he is a snake bae."

Me and Farriq locked eyes, and he just stared at me long and hard. He was probably thinking about everything I had just told him. My phone went off again with another text from Yas. This time, he was telling me how he was going to make me suck his dick until it was in my stomach; he was so rude.

"Can't that shit wait man!" Farriq snapped at me, eyeing my phone.

I nodded my head tapping the keys on the phone fast, so I could hurry up and place it back in my bag.

"My bad, bro. I met this sexy ass nigga at the bar my first night home. He from the north side and shit."

"The north side?" he asked, with a silly grin on his face. He knew like I knew, we didn't fuck with them, but it was something about Yas that had me willing to bend the rules a bit.

"Yeah, I know, I know, but I'm telling you, this nigga got a bitch willing to give him babies and shit. I ain't never met a nigga like Yas... not even Weezy, and yall niggas know I loved Weezy's aint shit ass. " I smiled wide and putting my phone away. When I looked up, I noticed Yajari and Farriq both looking at me like I was crazy.

"What?"

"Yas, as in Yassin?" asked Yajari. She had her face all frowned up, and she looked like she wanted to pop off or something. I didn't know what was up with this bitch. Just when I thought she was cool, she acts crazy again. Farriq really had his hands tied with her ass.

"What, yall know him or something?" I didn't wait for them to answer and continued talking about him.

"I know; he rude as hell and got a lil temper on him, but he cool peoples." I said, brushing them both off. Yajari hesitated for a minute, then said, "I know Yas. He's my brother."

"Yeah, okay."

"Nah, for real sis. That's her people. He one of those Abdul brothers. One of the twins." I looked to Yajari, and she dropped her head. It was the first time she actually showed any signs of selflessness since I met her.

"But. How? Ain't there like three brothers or some shit. They don't have any sisters-"

"It was a family secret. My father did that to protect me so our enemies wouldn't use me as a target. I'm the third 'brother', The Silent Assassin. Yas and my brother Sef are twins, and then I'm the oldest. The three of us ran the north side after my daddy gave his empire to us, but I met Farriq almost a year ago, and I didn't know he was the 'FJ' my family had beef with. By the time everything came out, I was already pregnant and my family pretty much disowned me. My brother Sef shot Farriq, and I shot Yas and his little bitch. After that, my father pretty much disowned me taking everything and leaving me for dead. He even put a hit out on me. I haven't spoken to my brothers in a few months."

I looked back and forth from Yajari to Farriq to see if they were playing, but they kept my gaze, and neither of them laughed or cracked a smile. Now that I looked at her real good, I could see the resemblance clear as day. She really did look like Yas, especially her eyes.

"Damn. I-I didn't even know. Your family really put a hit out on you while you were pregnant?" I asked, feeling sorry for her. Shit, I didn't have much family, but Farriq and his family had been all the family I ever needed. I don't know if I would have made it during my bid if I didn't have them. I may have cut everyone off, but Farriq kept money on my books and made sure no one fucked with me.

"I don't think it was so much my brothers, but I know it was my father. Either way, Yas and Sef betrayed me when they shot Farriq." She looked over to Farriq and smiled taking his hand. Right then, I could understand why they both went against the grain by messing with each other; they were in love.

"This shit is crazy." I mumbled to myself.

"Ayo, Court. I'm not gonna lie to you. This shit with Rashad is a little crazy to me. I'm a have my people look into it, though, and if it comes back that what you saying is true, are you prepared to-"

"FJ?" I said, calling him by his street name this time. He knew I meant business. "That nigga cost my best friend, Aida, and Arthur their wedding, and I lost six years of my life behind that rat ass nigga. I don't need you to do a mothafuckin thing; you know how I get down." I lifted my shirt to show him my 9 milli I had on my hip. "All I need is for you to stay out the way and back a nigga up. Ain't shit change in these streets, B,"

"You already know. Welcome back, my nigga." Me and Farriq both stood to our feet and hugged a brotherly hug. It felt good to be back and around my day one's. Yajari stood to her feet also, and we locked eyes just as me and Farriq separated.

"Look, Courtney. I know we started off on the wrong foot, and I can sometimes get a little crazy over the people I love. Farriq says you're family, so I have no choice but to accept that. I would also appreciate it, if you didn't tell Yas anything about Farriq or me. Right now, my focus is having a healthy pregnancy, and if I can't bust my gun, I rather just stay out the way."

I had to laugh at her, even though I knew she was serious. Shorty was a hot mess. Instead of saying anything back, I reached in and hugged her too. She was a little hesitant at first, but she loosened up a bit, and whether she believed it or not, I wasn't the hugging, mushy type either, but I was trying.

"My word is my bond, sis."

"Thank you, Courtney." After saying my goodbyes, I headed for the front door.

"Ay, I'm a get with you this week on some business shit. You back?" asked Farriq.

"Back like I never left."

****

After meeting with Farriq, I stopped by the liquor store on the boulevard and grabbed a bottle of Henny and a few Dutches. Yas and I were supposed to go to his crib and clean up the mess his bitch made after almost burning it down. Usually, this wouldn't even be my type of thing, but he asked, and I found myself saying yes. Fuck it.

As I was leaving out the liquor store, I passed Donnelly Homes, which were my old stomping grounds. Me, Farriq, and Rashad had that shit on smash back in the day. I remember staying up all night slanging crack in the halls, hustling until I broke day. There was one way in and one way out, unless you were walking, which had four entrances.

As I passed by my old building, I noticed a familiar face and slowed down parking by the entrance. It was Rashad. He was talking to a dark-skinned chick, and it looked like they were going back and forth about something. Shorty was using her hands to talk, like most the chicks around here did, and she was bouncing a little boy on her hip. He looked like he was only a couple of years old, but I didn't even know Rashad had a baby. Not that I would have been told by him anyway. Rashad looked like he was a few seconds off knocking her ass out, as he yoked her ass up against his car yelling in her face. I laughed to myself, because this nigga didn't even know how much he was slipping.

A few minutes later, Rashad and her kissed before he hopped in his car and headed out the complex towards my direction. Slouching down in my seat, I made sure he didn't see me because he had yet to know that I was home, and I wanted it to stay like that for now. When he was out of sight, I sat up, straight ready to pull off, but I noticed a black town car pull up, and the same shorty walked to the car still holding her baby.

I almost fell the fuck out when I saw Farriq climb out the back of the car and take the little boy out of her hands, before placing him in the car. She was trying to talk to him, but he barely said two words to her ass, then hopped back in the car and drove off.

Now ain't that some shit.

Farriq barely believed me when I told him about Rashad's snake ass, and from the looks of it, his ass was fucking Farriq's baby mother. Farriq had written me while I was in jail telling me he had a baby, but I never knew what he looked like. Now I did, and I couldn't believe this shit. Making a mental note, I started my car and pulled off, heading towards the parkway. I was trying to get my mind off of all the loyal people my bitch ass brother had crossed, so I turned my radio all the way up and drowned out the thoughts in my head telling me to turn around and kill they asses.

It took me about thirty minutes to get to Yas' gated community. There were big ass condo's that looked like they were houses, and each one had foreign cars in the driveways. After punching in the code he gave me, I followed the numbers on the houses to 802. Yas was sitting on the front porch, looking down on his phone, when I pulled into his driveway. By the time I stepped out the car holding my bags, he had finally looked up from his phone. His eyes met mine, and it was like the world had stopped at this exact moment.

"Hey beautiful,"

"Hey Handsome." I smiled back. Yas stood up and towered over me. He was looking sexy as hell dressed down in a pair of sweats, and a Polo V-neck. All whites were on his feet, and he had his dreads pulled back. Damn, he looked good as hell. He wrapped his arms around me and kissed me. For a minute, I forgot that we were outside, while I let his hands roam free up my fitted, white Polo shirt. His fingers traced over my nipples, and I threw my head back letting out a soft moan.

"Mmmm." I heard myself moan out. When I felt him

stop, I opened my eyes and he stood there wearing this cocky

grin.

"Why you stop?"

"Cause, we aren't here for that." he joked, grabbing my

hand and leading the way into his home.

"Alright, I'm a remember that."

"Don't trip, Ma. I got you." he smiled. We walked

inside, and I was shocked to see how most of the ceiling and the

whole upper part of the house were gone. I mean it didn't look

that bad from the outside, but the inside was fucked all the way

up.

"Oh my, God. That bitch did all of this? What the fuck

did she do! Pour propane around this bitch?" I was literally in

shock at this shit. Looking at what used to be a beautiful home,

I was about ready to go and fuck her ass up myself. I know I

was the one she probably blamed, but everything was

completely ruined.

"They say she lit the bedroom blinds on fire and shit. That bitch a little off, but I mean, it is what it is. I ain't gotta deal with her shit no more, and she ain't gotta deal with mine. Bitch tried to tell me she was pregnant and shit." My eyes squinted when he said the word pregnant.

"Chill, Ma. Her ass ain't pregnant. Her ass had pads in the trash can and shit like I was born yesterday. Like I don't know women. She a fucking trip."

"I would say I don't know why, but I guess I do."

"Is that right?" A wicked grin popped on my face, but I said nothing.

After he handed me a big black garbage bag and some gloves, we began to trash everything in the kitchen and foyer. We were both silently cleaning, while the sounds of Yo Gotti bounced throughout the house. I glanced back and noticed Yas leaning against the couch rolling up a blunt. That made me stop and smirk at him; he was such a pothead.

"How you gonna have me up in here cleaning by myself." I fake pouted.

Yas smirked never taking his eyes off the weed he was breaking down in his hands.

"A nigga started getting mad all over again seeing my shit like this. I needed a little pick me up," he said laughing. I dropped the almost filled garbage bag and pulled off my gloves while I approached him.

"So what you gonna now?" I asked.

"As far as what? My house?"

"Yeah. I mean… you do have insurance or something, right?"

"Hell yeah!" he boasted, finally looking up at me. I was sitting next to him now. My hand covered my laugh, and I cracked up at his animated response.

"Shorty, if that bitch would've burnt my crib down, and I had no insurance, we would be digging her hole in the back right now. Fuck that."

"We?" my eyebrow raised up. Yas did a subtle shrug, right before lighting the end of the blunt up.

"Yeah. WE. You ain't gotta front for me, Ma, I know the real you. You ain't no stranger to shootouts and dumping bodies. You was like the Griselda Blanca of South Jersey and shit." I fell out laughing again. He was funny as hell even though he didn't try; it came naturally. That's why we clicked so much.

"You so stupid," I nudged him on the shoulder. Yas inhaled the big cloud of smoke and then passed it to me. I leaned back on the sofa and took a long, deep pull letting the weed take over my mind, body, and soul.

I could feel him move closer to me and throw his arm across my back, as if we were on a date at the movies. We were silent. It was just us, Yo Gotti, and the Kush.

"Ay. Court, can I ask you something?"

"Hmm?"

I handed him his blunt back and closed my eyes resting my head back against the sofa. The weed was potent as hell, and even with the few pulls I had, I was high as a kite. They didn't have this type of weed out here before I went in, so I was still adjusting. Yas hesitated for a second, and I opened up my eyes to look at him closely.

What the fuck he want to say, I thought snidely.

"Wh-Why... why you never talk about your brother? I mean, you know I know who you are, and I'm sure you know I got beef with that nigga, but why you never even mention him?" I sat dumbfounded for a minute at the line of questioning. Why would Yas want me to bring Rashad's name up anyway? Was this a setup? He sensed my tenseness and let out an exasperated laugh.

"Ma, relax. I ain't on no bullshit. Look where you at. I wouldn't have brought you here. I'm just. I'm so intrigued by you. You're different than them other girls. I wanna know everything there is to know about you. No secrets." I sat up and sighed a little.

"There's nothing to really tell. If you know about me, then I'm sure you know about my brother. Every dog has their day. Rashad being my brother doesn't make him exempt from that." He didn't reply back. Instead, he took another toke off the blunt nodding his head in an understanding way.

I stood up and walked further into the living room to take a good look around at what was left. There was a nice, plush carpet, a big, flat screen TV that looked like it still worked, and a few paintings hung on the wall.

Pictures of Yajari sat above the mantle all over, along with another guy who he resembled. I was guessing that was his twin brother, Sef. They all looked happy, and it seemed like they were really close to each other, but like they say, a picture was worth a thousand words.

"Who's this?" I asked, pointing to a picture of just Jari.

Yajari asked me to not mention Farriq or her, and I would keep my word. She didn't have to worry about me on no shady shit, because I didn't get down like that. I would however be nosey, since he was inquiring about my sibling. Yas walked over to where I was and looked at the photo. I could tell by the look in his eyes, he loved his sister and was hurt.

"Someone I hurt really bad who was really close to my heart. You probably won't get to meet her, though, cause I fucked up real bad with her, but I mean, it is what it is, I guess." He solemnly said. The hurt in his eyes was evident when he spoke, and I knew right then he loved his sister. I know it was supposed to be a natural thing, however look at the shit me and Rashad were going through.

Stepping closer to Yas, I laid my head on his shoulder while he stared back at the picture frame of Jari. She was cheesing hard as hell and had a cap on her head with the tassel at the side; I could tell it was her graduation pictures.

"Well…" I started, slowly. "If you know it was your fault and you fucked up… maybe you should apologize. You know sometimes people underestimate the power of an apology. I can tell by the way you look at her picture she is someone worth fighting for."

He shook his head, "Too much shit has happened, though, you know? I don't even know where I would begin, feel me?"

"Do you know where she is?"

"Nah…" he said. "And after the way me and my family did her, I don't blame her for getting ghost on our ass."

Damn. This nigga looked like he was about to burst into tears right now. I don't know all that happened between Yas and his sister, but I knew the love outweighed it all. It took everything inside of me not to call Farriq up and hash this shit out now, but I gave my word, and unlike others, my word was my bond, so instead, I left it alone and let our silence fill the room.

For the first time since meeting Yas, I felt more than just a physical connection to him. What started off as just sex was slowly but surely blossoming into more? At first, it frightened me... the thought of loving another man and being vulnerable to him. But the more Yas spoke, and opened up to me, the more I trusted my instincts to love him back.

I couldn't say I loved him yet, but I was in deep like. I was willing to ride this shit for now, and if he crossed me... I'd just have to bury his ass right next to Rashad

Chapter 10

Youusef

Life had a funny way of working out, I was starting to see. From the moment we are born, we are brought in a world full of chaos then after years of being sheltered, we're thrown back out there to fend for ourselves. No one had told me that being a twin was this hard or that I would be faced with constant dilemmas.

It was going on three months now, since I had been shot or had last saw my sister, and even though I was acting like shit was good, it was fucking me up day by day. I could never pick up the phone or find the words to say to her when I called her, though. Although I was upset at her choosing her nigga's side, I couldn't help but be more disappointed in myself for how I handled things.

Sitting in my den, I was nursing a shot of Henny, while I stared at a picture of Yas, Jari, and myself. We had taken it last year at the amusement part for Jari's birthday. Jari had always been a daredevil, and her ass lived for rollercoasters and all types of stomach dropping shit, so last year for her birthday, Yas and I surprised her with all-inclusive tickets to Dorney Park. We had a ball that day, and even looking back at the pictures, it caused a smile to creep on my face.

"Mommy, when can we go and see auntie again? I miss her sooooo much; it's been forever." Alia said.

"Shhhhh, Lia."

I could hear Rosa attempting to hush her from the kitchen, but it was too late. I was already on my feet and walking in. Rosa looked up at me standing in the doorway, her face flushed red from being busted.

"You saw Yajari? Why you ain't tell me Rosa?"

"We see her all the time, Daddy! Mommy said we have to be careful when I give her my bear hugs though, because she 'pegnant'. She's having a baby, Daddy!" Alia's motor mouth said.

Alia was good for spilling everything; she couldn't hold water if she tried. Rosa stood there staring at Alia shaking her head. She was standing on the opposite side of the center island cutting up some potatoes for our dinner. Alia stood beside her with a matching apron on, using her kitchen play set toys to pretend like she was cutting up food too. Rosa and I locked eyes for a minute, my jaw tightened, and I thought about slapping the fuck out of her ass for lying to me all this time.

"Alia, go get ready for dinner."

"Okay, Mommy." Once she was out of earshot, I walked over to Rosa with a slight limp.

"So we hiding shit now? Why you ain't tell me you been

seeing Jari! You know we haven't seen or heard from her in

months, and you haven't said shit." I gritted.

Rosa's arched eyebrows turned up at me slightly.

"First of all, why the fuck wouldn't I speak to my sister?

I never hide a damn thing; I just never mentioned it to your

ignorant ass. I've been trying to stay out of it, but since you

want to talk about it now, let's." She placed the knife down on

the counter top, and her perfectly manicured hands were now on

her hips. Rosa snapped her neck around looking ghetto as hell,

and I wanted to burst out laughing at her, but I couldn't because

she would probably fuck my ass up in here.

"You need to apologize to Yajari."

"Mannn…"

"I'm not finished!" she shot. "You need to apologize to

your sister, Youssef. This mess with you three has been going

on long enough, and honestly, I'm sick of the shit. In four

months, your sister is going to be a mother. Can you look me in the face and tell me you don't give a fuck about your niece or nephew? This bullshit has gone too fucking far, and I'm sick of this shit! Yall were wrong, Youusef. You, Yas, and even your parents. Yall all are dead wrong for what you're doing to that girl, and you know it!"

"She chose sides!"

"Well, YOU made her!!" Rosa yelled back at me.

I massaged my chin, trying to calm myself down. Rosa and Jari had always been close so it wasn't much of a shocker that Rosa was going in on me about the shit. I'm actually surprised she hadn't done it sooner.

"I'm going to have a dinner... and Yajari and Farriq are both invited-"

"I'm not sitting down eating dinner wit that nigga. You can kill that shit, Ma. It's not happening, and you know damn well Yas ain't coming to that shit either." Rosa ran her tongue across the front of her teeth then clicked her tongue.

"Well, I suggest you change his mind then huh?" she piqued. I stared at her long and hard for a minute. Where the hell was all this shit coming from?

"Rosa. Why the fuck you care so much? You know as well as I do, that nigga Farriq don't fuck with us Abdul's. You want me to admit that I was wrong, okay, I was wrong, but that shit don't change the fact that she shot Yas! Or that she betrayed my father's empire. She's just as much wrong as we are! And what's crazy is you standing there defending that bitch, like she didn't almost have YOUR husband killed!"

Rosa sighed loudly and walked closer to me. She reached her hand up to my face and ran her fingers down it, then out of nowhere, she slapped the shit out of me. It stung like hell, but I refrained from hitting her ass back.

"Don't you sass me, Youusef! I care because this family is the ONLY fucking family that I have! I care because, ever since you and Yas been beefing with Jari, shit ain't been right! A house divided will fall, nigga, and I'm part of this house too!"

Rosa spat at me. "I wasn't there; I can't defend anyone, but what I can do is make sure that the man I married isn't a prideful asshole and rights his wrongs. Everyone is constantly blaming her when she had no idea who he was. The minute she found out who he was, she immediately told him that, if he came for any of you, she would kill him."

"Jari had your family's back from the very beginning and y'all shitted on her. We both know if Farriq really wanted you dead, he has the avenues to be able to do just like you and Yas do…The fact that he hasn't goes to show he must not have been beefing off you too much."

She was mad as hell right now, and I wasn't really trying to take it there with her, but she did make sense. Rosa knew she couldn't beat me, but her ass would use everything up in here to try. I was willing to try and compromise with her. I sucked my teeth and leaned up against the counter using my elbows.

"What do you want me to do bae?" I finally asked.

"I want you to be on your best behavior when I invite Yajari and Farriq here. And don't tell Yas they are coming either." Rosa stated. She picked up the knife from off the counter and resumed cutting the potatoes.

They always said Spanish women were crazy, and every year that I been married to Rosa, I was beginning to see that it was truth to that statement.

"What if she doesn't come?"

Rosa nodded proudly and said, "She will… because I'm going to ask her. And Jari loves me." I didn't say another word; I just gave her my back and headed back out the kitchen. If Rosa thought she could get us all in the same room without bullets flying…that was fine by me; she could be my guest.

******

A week later, I was putting on the slacks and button down Rosa had assembled for me. I wasn't sure how she was able to pull it off, but Jari had agreed to come to dinner at our house, and it was tonight. For some odd reason, I was nervous as a black nigga getting pulled over by the police. Maybe it was because I hadn't seen my sister in a few months, or it could have been because I didn't know what to expect, but on the real, a nigga was feeling butterflies and shit like it was the first time that I had met Rosa.

Standing in the mirror, I slipped my Gucci loafers on my feet. Rosa had picked out a salmon-colored shirt and some slacks for me to wear. The gold studded out diamond bezel Rolex sparkled when the lights hit it, and I was feeling like my old self again. There was still a slight limp when I walked, but I wasn't in as much pain that I had been. Tucking my nine in my pants, I didn't even hear Rosa walk up behind me with a mean mug on her face.

"What now Rosa?" I asked, growing annoyed.

"Why do you have that gun? Aren't we just eating?"

"You can never be too careful baby girl." She rolled her eyes and attempted to walk away, but I caught her hand and pulled her back towards me.

Holding her in my arms, I nuzzled my mouth between the crook of her neck inhaling her signature scent. Rosa was looking good as hell in a fitted, cream-colored dress that stopped mid-thigh, hugging her slim thick figure with her small belly sticking out. Her long hair was pulled back in a messy French braid, and she had little-to-no makeup on her face. She was glowing.

"You look beautiful bae." I said, in between kisses.

"Mhhmmm… you just make sure you're on your best behavior tonight."

"I am… Can I get some pussy?"

Rosa blushed like an innocent schoolgirl when I said that. She had been holding out on a nigga all week to see if I was going to flunk out on this dinner party. Good thing she had, because I was really planning on not being here either. My hand went to her visible baby bump, and I rubbed it while still kissing on her neck softly.

"You really not gonna give me none of this… you know how much I love your pussy when you pregnant…mmm, you smell good."

Rosa smiled wide, "Like what?"

"Like….Goya beans." I burst out laughing hard as hell, and Rosa pushed me back off her. She couldn't help but laugh at me being silly.

"You so stupid. I'll meet you downstairs." She said, kissing my lips once more.

I took a piss then joined her downstairs in the dining room. Alia was sitting on the couch, in the den on her tablet, while Rosa set the table with her fine China. She could act like this shit was all about us if she wanted, but I know her ass loves hosting dinner parties, and that was the real reason behind all of this. I was leaning against the doorframe, admiring her beauty when the doorbell rang.

"Babe, get that for me. I'm going to go and start putting the food out."

Nodding, I headed to the front door. On the other side stood Yas and a chocolate beauty, they both were so into kissing they didn't even see me standing there until I cleared my throat.

"AHEM!"

"Oh, shit…" Yas laughed, wiping his mouth. "My bad, brah, What's good witcha?" he said, dapping me up. Yas turned to the chick and said, "Court, this my brother Youusef. Sef, this my shorty, Courtney."

"What's up?" I greeted, taking her hand before shaking it.

Once the introductions were over, we then stepped inside heading to the living room. I walked behind them both, and I couldn't help but notice the ass shorty was carrying behind her. She was a lot different from Chi; she wore her hair in big curls and it reached the middle of her back, and instead of an expensive dress and heels, she opted for an all-black maxi dress, with some gold sandals on. The closer I looked, the more familiar she began to look. Then the name Courtney, struck a bell.

"Uncleeeeeee!" Alia squealed. As usual, she jumped up in his arms kissing her favorite uncle on the cheek. Yas smiled wide, hugging her back.

"What's up niece?"

"Where's that other girl?" Alia asked, sizing up Courtney.

I took Alia nosey self out of Yas' hands and called for Rosa. She came out the kitchen a second later wearing that contagious smile of hers.

"What up sis?"

"Heyyy, brother. You look good."

Rosa and Yas hugged, while I stood off to the side holding Alia. She wasn't really feeling the idea of her uncle having a new girlfriend.

"Sis, I want you to meet my shorty Courtney. Court, this my sister-in-law, but she more blood to me than anything." Rosa blushed, then took Courtney's hand smiling.

"It's nice to meet you, Rosa. Yas told me a lot about you. All of you. Your home is beautiful."

"Aw thanks girl." Rosa said.

"Uh, bae, you mind taking Alia real quick while I holla at Yas?"

Rosa shot me an unsure look, as did Yas. They knew I had something to speak on, but I wasn't about to put him on front street like that. The last family dinner we had, Chi let us know she was swinging from a pole and shit. Yas didn't say much on it, but I know it bothered him.

"Uh yeah. Courtney, can you help me finish putting out the rest of the food. We have more guests coming."

"Of course, no problem. Shit, this is probably going to be the closest I get to a kitchen anyways." Courtney said laughing.

"You can't cook?" I asked. It came out a little harsher than I expected, and Rosa gave me a slight nudge.

"Depends on what we talking about cooking?"

Courtney gave me a raised eyebrow, and Yas burst out laughing. I even had to laugh at how smooth the chick was; it was funny. She reminded me of a female Yas.

Rosa took Alia out my hands, and she and Courtney headed into the kitchen leaving the two of us alone. Soon as they were gone, his defenses kicked in.

"Don't start, Sef."

"So you fucking with the enemy now too huh?"

"It ain't like that... this is different. I think she's the one brah." Yas said. He was cheesing wide again, and it made me chuckle a little bit. I took a long sigh and placed my hands on the top of my head.

"We grown, Yas. I can't tell you who to like, feel me? I'm not about to get in the middle of anyone's love life any more. Just make sure you're careful, and watch ya back aight?"

Yas and I locked eyes, and he nodded sincerely. With all the shit going on with our family, I couldn't handle my twin getting himself caught up behind no bitch. I wouldn't be able to take it.

"She good brah. Shorty got my back and I got her front. You wouldn't understand me if I tried to tell you-" he shook his head in disbelief. "It's something about her yo."

"I bet there is... she the female you." I said, laughing. Yas looked towards the kitchen with the same dumb ass look on his face again.

"She is right?"

Aw, man. This nigga was in love. He didn't even have to say it; my twin connection let me know that shit. I nodded my head and threw my arm around him laughing.

"You got your work cut out for you baby brother."

"We both do."

We stepped back inside, and I saw both Rosa and Courtney coming out the kitchen bringing the food in the dining room. Alia was in her own little world with that damn iPad, so

157

Rosa had everybody sit down, and just as we were about to say grace, the doorbell rang. She and I both looked at each other while Yas gave me a confused look, and Courtney was on her phone.

"Excuse me, guys. I'll be right back." Rosa said and moved her chair back. I watched her step out the room. I heard some voices, and Alia must've known who it was, because she jumped up from the table.

"Auntieeeeeee." She screamed, and Yas looked at me.

"Man, it was all Rosa." I had my hands up.

Yajari walked in the room, and it was complete silence. She scanned the room first, and when her eyes landed on Yas, she started tearing up and walked out. The dude FJ followed behind her. I stood up to walk out, and I could hear her saying she was ready to leave.

"Jari, you knew it was a possibility they would be here. This is your brother's house."

"I know, but-"

"Jari, cut it out. You missed both of them, and now you're all here. Baby, get yourself together, and go back in there. If you don't want to talk then fine, but I don't want to hear you whining later about what you should've or could've said." She nodded her head up and down as he wiped her face. Damn, both of my siblings were finally feeling how it is to be in love. It's just crazy to witness them with a known enemy, but they say opposites attract like a motherfucker.

Chapter 11

Yajari

Rosa called me the other day asking me to come by for dinner and told me that I could bring Farriq. The two of them hit it off well, and I appreciate that, being he was going to be in my life forever now. I wasn't really comfortable being around Sef right now, but I'd rather him than Yas. I don't think I could get over him putting his hands on me just like I was sure he wasn't able to forgive me for shooting him. Imagine my surprise when I got to Rosa's, and he was sitting in the dining room with Courtney. I turned around, and Farriq came behind me. He wouldn't allow me to leave and was right there to comfort me like always.

"But Farriq, I don't want to see him."

"Jari, go back in there and stop acting like a baby." I folded my arms and stood there. He pulled me in closer and wiped my eyes.

"Jari, I'm going to eat that pussy real good when we get home if you do this." He whispered in my ear, and I let a grin creep on my face.

"Look at your horny ass."

"What? It's been two days."

"I told you I'm nervous about having sex now that you're getting bigger."

"Well then, we can just wait until I deliver. And just so you know, it's another six weeks after that." I told him and went to walk away.

"Stop playing, Jari. You know damn well I'm not waiting that long. Let's get through this dinner so you can go for a ride. I know that's all you really want." He said softly so Sef couldn't hear us since I saw him standing there waiting.

"Whatever." I wiped the little bit of tears I had left and turned around to ask Farriq if I looked ok. He was staring down at his phone with a frown. I was going to question him but I didn't. Sef was staring a hole in me as I headed in his direction to get back in the dining room.

"Come here, Yajari." He said and reached out for me. I glanced at Farriq, and he nodded his head. Not that he was giving me permission, but more for me speaking to him. Sef walked out, and I followed behind him on the back porch. All I kept thinking about was leaving him with Yas, but then again, Courtney was in there, too, and I knew she wasn't about to let anything happen.

"How are you Jari?" He asked as he leaned on the house.

"Sef, I miss you so much. When Daddy disowned me, I had to get away. I never thought we would ever go this long without speaking. I just want my brother back and-" He hushed me and gave me a hug. Neither of us wanted to let go.

"Jari, I know you were mad, but you didn't have to stop speaking to me. I didn't even do anything."

"I know, but I just cut everyone off. I felt like no one loved me but Farriq, and-" I saw his face get right when I said that.

"It doesn't matter what happened; you're my sister, and I will never turn my back on you." He lifted my head up and handed me a tissue that Rosa just came out with. I didn't even know she was standing there.

"I didn't know, Sef. Daddy said I was cut off, and I heard that you were shot, then I shot Yas, and everything was crazy, and it's all my fault because I should've told you who I was dealing with. I'm sorry about everything. Rosa. I don't think this was a good idea." I tried to leave, but she stepped in front of me and told me to stop running away.

"Stop it, Jari. No one is mad at you. You're rambling on, and not once did you hear me blame you for anything. Ok, you didn't tell us about him, but you can't help who you fell in love with. I'm not happy about it, but from the looks of things, he definitely loves the hell out of you. I mean, he came to the house of his worst enemy alone for you. That shit means something." He said, as he lifted my head and wiped my face again.

"Sef, I shot my brother over a man. We have never allowed anyone to come between us."

"And it won't happen again." I heard Yas say behind me. I turned around, and he was standing there with his hands in his pants. The two of us just stared until he reached out and hugged me. I cried so hard in his arms he had to push me back to make sure I was ok. He kissed my cheek and hugged me again.

"Auntie, are you ok?" I heard my niece say when she came out. I moved back from Yas and looked at her.

"Yes, I'm fine honey. Can you tell Farriq I'll be in there in a few?"

"I will, but he's trying to catch a Pokemon on my iPad for me in the front." We all started laughing when she said that.

Last week, when Rosa brought her over, he downloaded the game for her and took her to the park and other places to find them. Believe it or not, she loves her some Farriq and she can do no wrong in his eyes.

"Yas, I'm sorry." I finally said.

"Stop, Jari. I should be the one apologizing. There was no reason I should have put my hands on you. You had every right to defend yourself. I saw the hurt and pain in your eyes for me and him when you did it, and I'm sorry that I was the one who made you do it. I love you so much, and the only thing that kept me from looking for you was him. I saw the love both of you had for one another and knew you were safe if you were together."

"I was, and his father has me under his protection now that your parents disowned me." I told them and asked Rosa for more tissues. I couldn't stop crying as I sat in between both of them on the bench outside. The three of us stayed out there for a good ten minutes still apologizing to one another. Yas explained to me how hurt he was that I had really shot him, and when he told me about his recovery I felt even more fucked up. This whole thing was some real life time shit. They both seemed excited when I told them I was having a boy. Farriq wanted a girl since he had a son already, but this would be the first for us in our family.

"You feel better baby." Farriq asked me on our way home. After my brothers and I went inside, Rosa made us eat. She said she didn't cook all that food for nothing. My brothers spoke among themselves while the rest of us conversed. I didn't expect any different between any of them and I wasn't mad. When it was time for me to leave, we all exchanged hugs, and I told them I expected to see them at my baby shower.

"I do, but I can't help but think about how I almost killed my brother."

"Jari, if you wanted to kill him, you could have, and we all know that. Stop beating yourself up over something that can't be undone. You discussed it, forgave one another, and now it's time to move on. If you continue focusing on it, you won't ever move past it."

"You're so good to me." I told him when the driver finally pulled up to the house. I scooted over to get out on the same side as him. He hated that I did that. I shut the door and followed him inside.

"This is what you want right?" He closed the door and tossed me against the wall gently. He kissed on my neck hungrily and pulled my shirt over my head. I unsnapped my bra letting my breasts spill out and he attacked them like a hungry animal. The way he sucked on and flickered over them had my body ready to feel him inside me.

"I want my dick now." I whispered and started unbuckling his jeans.

"Nah, you want that pussy ate first." He pulled my pants and panties down and helped me step out of them. He sat on the chair we had in the foyer that came with that small ass table we put our mail on and lifted my leg.

"Yes, baby. Fuck I missed this." I moaned out as he sucked on my pearl and allowed two of his fingers go in and find my g-spot.

"Cum for me, Jari. I'm thirsty."

"Oh Goddddddd." I let two days' worth come out, and he sucked all of my juices up. I kneeled down and took his dick out. Then, I placed him in my mouth and sucked his soul out. I had him grabbing the chair as he came hard.

"You know I'm about to fuck the hell out of you?" He asked stroking himself as I bent over in front of him.

"I wouldn't have it any other way right now. Fuck me, Farriq." I said, and he entered me roughly and had me screaming and trying to get away. His dick was not small, and he always left me with a grin on my face and a sore pussy.

****

The next day, I woke up to him yelling at someone on the phone. I looked up and his back was turned but I could see how mad he was in the mirror. Once he hung the phone up, I wrapped my arms around him and let my hands find his man who was soft as hell. I started stroking him but he stopped me.

"Not right now, Jari."

"Are you ok?" I asked, and he put his head down. "Farriq, what's wrong?"

"Nothing Jari, damn."

"Why are you talking to me like that?"

"If I tell you nothing is wrong, just listen."

"Excuse me. I wake up to hear my man arguing with someone, and I'm the bad guy for trying to relieve some of that stress."

"It's not that. When a man is mad, just let him be."

"Ok, but you weren't mad at me. But fuck it, I'll leave you the fuck alone. I won't say shit to you." I backed up and put my hands up.

"Jari?"

"Nope. I'm good. I don't know who spoiled your day, but you're not going to take that shit out on me." I grabbed my towel and jumped in the shower. I washed up and let the water rinse the soap off. I felt the cold wind and knew it was him getting in and I stepped out. I wasn't in the mood to be anywhere around him. I tried to rush and get dressed but he came out as I started putting some pants on.

"Jari?"

"I'm over it, Farriq."

"Let me talk to you." He said as I was walking out the door.

"You should've done that instead of snapping on me."

"Where are you going?"

"None of your fucking business. Worry about that person on the phone."

"Don't get fucked up trying to be tough."

"Fuck you." I yelled out and walked to one of the cars. I heard him slam the front door behind me. I didn't want anyone driving me so I sat in in the Lexus truck and waited for the garage door to open. I saw the door open from inside, then he started walking to the truck and I pulled off. I had no destination

in mind. Twenty minutes later, I ended up at the mall. Retail

therapy was the answer for any woman. I checked my purse to

make sure I had the bank card, and sure enough, I did.

I stayed in the mall for a couple of hours browsing and

purchasing some things for the baby and me. I didn't buy him

shit nor did I feel bad spending his money. What I did feel some

kind of way about is me having to depend on him like he was

my father. Now that I spoke to my brothers, I had to find out if

they could get me some work without my father finding out.

"Yup, that's the bitch." I heard behind me. At first, I

wasn't going to turn around, because there's no way they were

speaking of me. I knew no one down here.

"Why are you mad at her though? She doesn't even

know about the two of you." Now, that shit right there caught

my attention. I didn't think Farriq was cheating. I mean, how

could he? We were always together, but then again, that doesn't

mean shit. Look at what happened with my brother and Rosa. If a man's going to cheat, he'll find a way.

"He better hurry up and tell her. I'm tired of hiding our relationship and this baby won't be a secret. I don't care who she is." I turned around and stared at some chick who looked like she saw a ghost.

"I'm sorry, but are you talking about my man? Before you say no, I would prefer you not lie."

"What?" She answered like she didn't know I was talking to her.

"It seems that the two of you were discussing a man that's cheating on his woman. I can only assume you're talking of mine if you decided to have your conversation directly behind me." The friend put her head down to look at her phone and started laughing. I stared at the other one waiting on her to speak. She was a very pretty woman, and I could see her being his type. She was dressed in expensive clothes, her hair was well kept, and she definitely had a glow around her body.

"If your man's name is Farriq Coy, then yes, I am

talking about him."

"Oh, ok. So what? You wanted me to find out about this little affair you claim to be having with him right?" She shook her head yes and gave me a fake smile.

"You told me, so now what? You expect me to start crying or even start cursing you out?" She rolled her eyes. "I'm letting you know that's not going to happen. But what's not going to happen again is you coming to me on some childish shit. If you know who I am, then approaching me as a woman is where you should've started. Second, if Farriq is who you want, then honey have at it. I'm not into keeping a man who doesn't want to be kept. And if you're sleeping with him like you say, then he's not really my man, now is he?" She stood there stuck on stupid.

"Damn, she just let your ass have it in a nice way." Her friend said laughing.

"I'm just saying that we been sleeping together for a while now, and I no longer want him part-time." I threw my head back laughing at her.

"Honey, is that what you signed up for? Because if you did, I hate to tell you that if he hired you for a part-time position, you can bet there's more with that same spot." Her mouth fell open.

"You women kill me. I get that you don't owe me shit because we just met, but if you were aware he had a woman and continued sleeping with him, it just makes you look like the side chick who thinks fucking him good will make you the main chick. But what y'all don't realize is a man will not wife a ho. What you're doing with him he's going to assume you did with another, therefore you won't have a secure spot in his life. I know women love the competition, but sweetie they always choose the wife, unless they were unhappy prior to you, and even then, he will still pick someone else." I picked my bags up and attempted to walk off.

"I know who you are, Yajari Abdul, and everyone knows your father disowned you. Farriq doesn't want a broke

174

bitch that sits around the house all day doing nothing." I was so mad, but I had to contain my anger in this mall. I stepped in her face.

"If you know me, then you know I will kill you the second you step foot out this mall, get in my truck, and go home and fuck the shit out of the man you claim to with. Bitch, don't come for me because you won't win."

"Let's go, Patrice. Why would you bring that shit up to her? It doesn't matter where she is. Someone is always watching and protecting her. You're fucking stupid. Let's go." I heard her friend say and grab her arm. I stood there smirking as she let her friend pull her away. My phone started ringing, and it was Farriq. I allowed him to go to voicemail. I went to an ATM and took out six hundred dollars since that's all you can withdraw then went inside the bank to withdraw more. Then, I remembered the card only had his name on it. I picked my phone up and called my brother Yas.

"What's up, Jari?" He said in the phone like he was out

of breath.

"Um, I know this is crazy to ask you, but have you seen Courtney around? I need to ask her something." I heard some noise in the background, and she got on the phone.

"Jari. Is everything ok?"

"Yea, everything's fine. Is there somewhere you can meet me?"

"Right now, Jari?" I heard Yas yelling in the background.

"Yas be quiet." She told him and I laughed.

"Sure, where do you want to meet?"

"I'll be out that way in forty minutes, you tell me?"

"I stay at a hotel right now, so it's ok if you come here."

"Hell no, Court. We're not done. I knew I should've let her blocking ass go to voicemail."

"Tell Yas I can hear him, and I won't be long. He can have you before I get there and after I leave with his nasty ass." Courtney started laughing, and I could hear him suck his teeth.

It seemed like the two of them were more than just fuck buddies if you ask me. She gave me the name of the hotel she was at and told me to have the front desk let her know when I was there. I started the truck up and hopped on the parkway.

Chapter 12

Farriq

My phone ringing off the hook this morning woke me
up, and I didn't mean to be as loud as I was. I also didn't mean
to snap on Jari the way I did either. I was in love with her, there
was no mistaken that. Unfortunately, the day she left the house
when I found out who she was and came back to find Tish
sucking my dick, I thought we were finished. Therefore, those
two weeks of not speaking to her led someone else into my bed.
It wasn't right, but we weren't together. One night I was venting
to my boy Rashad about how I couldn't get Jari off my mind,
and he took me out thinking it would help. It did, but I picked
the wrong bitch to take home, that's for damn sure.

"Patrice, this is Farriq. Farriq, this is Patrice." Rashad
said, introducing us, and I gave him a crazy look. Since when

178

has this nigga told a female my government name? I was going to check his ass about that shit later.

Anyway, Patrice was beautiful all the way around. She was light-skinned with long, red hair flowing down her back. Her breasts had to be somewhere in the D section and her ass was nice and fat. She didn't have a stomach, and she had a decent set of teeth on her. When she spoke, I could tell she wasn't ghetto or at least it didn't seem like it. As the night went on, the drinks continued coming and I was becoming overly intoxicated. I told Rashad I was leaving, and this nigga, who was the designated driver claimed he was too messed up to drive and offered Patrice to take me home. He was bugging knowing I didn't bring chicks to my house, but I was so fucked up I just went with the flow.

"This is a nice house, Farriq." She said and closed the door behind me. I turned around to speak, and she had her tongue down my throat and was unbuckling my pants at the same time. I'm not even going to lie and say I fought her off

179

because I didn't. I wasn't with Jari anymore, and I wanted to fuck, plain and simple. I remember her sucking my dick and me telling her to be quiet when I had her ass bent over by the stairs screaming.

Needless to say, the next day, I woke up in my bed with her next to me. Again, I didn't think anything of it until I looked at myself and saw dried up cum on me. I prayed it was my own from a condom but I didn't remember.

"Hey sexy." She came into the bathroom with me, reached over, and stroked my man back to life. I took her back to the bedroom, grabbed a condom, and fucked her a few times before she left. She and I hooked up a couple more times after that. The day I was shot she was supposed to meet me back at my house, and of course, it didn't happen. When I was released from the hospital, Jari and I were back together and my phone number was changed. Once I moved to my father's place I wasn't worried about her popping up because she was only aware of the old one I stayed in.

Last week, I went to see Rashad before I knew Courtney was home and she told me all that shit, and he told me that he ran into Patrice and gave her my number. I wasn't mad, because no one knew I was back with Jari yet. However, I couldn't change my number when I had just gotten this one. The first time she texted me was yesterday at the dinner over Jari's brother's house. She told me she was pregnant, and that the baby was mine. I couldn't say she was lying due to it being a strong possibility. I told her to hit me up when she delivered.

The bitch sent messages to my phone all night so I blocked her. This morning she called me from a different number, and I thought it was someone calling about business because she was calling back to back. I answered, and she said that, if I didn't come see her, she would tell my girl about the baby. I planned on telling Jari, because we were broken up, but she left. I didn't mean to yell, but between Patrice and this Rashad shit, I had a lot going on. I called her phone a few times, but she sent me to voicemail each time.

I walked out to the truck, and my driver told me he got a call that Jari was on her way up north. She was followed everywhere she went and her whereabouts were always known to me. I had him take me to Rashad's house because I needed to find out, without saying much, if what Courtney spoke about was true. When the driver pulled up, he came out the house and gave me a brotherly hug, then invited me in. I asked where his girl was and he said they broke up because she was tired of catching him cheating. I couldn't blame her though. Rashad loved getting pussy but he wanted that wife at home and she wasn't hearing it.

"Hey Rashad. Hey Farriq." I heard some chick say when she came in the house. I had no idea who she was but I spoke anyway. I stood up and grabbed a beer out his fridge and heard the person I didn't want to asking could she speak to me in the other room. I blew my breath out and took slow steps in there like I was about to get in trouble. I thought she was in the living room, but she wasn't. I knocked on the bathroom door and she told me to come in. I opened it and she was on the toilet. I

backed up to give her privacy.

"Don't leave."

"What? You're using the bathroom."

"I want you to see something." She lifted a white stick

from under her and sat it on the counter on some tissue. She

cleaned herself up and washed her hands. I watched the line go

from nothing to two pink lines. I leaned back on the door and

closed my eyes for a minute. I had to come to grips with

possibly having three baby mothers. The only one I wanted to

birth the rest of my kids was damn sure going to leave me if this

child was mine. I may not have cheated on her, but I should've

been a lot smarter.

"Patrice, I don't know how I slipped up, but honestly, I

don't want a kid with you. I know it's your body and you can

do what you want, but if you decide to keep it, I will be

involved in the child's life and that's it. You and I are not going

to be together." The chick dropped to her knees and fuck me for wearing sweatpants. She was able to get them down along with my boxers in no time. I felt her warm mouth around my dick and instantly got hard.

"Shit, Patrice. Damn girl." I called out. I had no business allowing this woman to give me head when I had one at home.

"You like the way I suck it, Farriq."

"Nah, my girl does it way better." I told her and pulled it out her mouth. I was still hard, and it was feeling good, but I loved my girl too much to let her finish. I lifted my sweats and boxers up and opened the door. I saw the chick he was with snapping pictures of her and Rashad. I gave him dap and told him I would see him later. I needed to remove myself from the situation before things went left. I called Jari again when I got back to the house and this time she answered.

"Yes, Farriq."

"Are you coming home?" She laughed and I looked at my phone to make sure I wasn't bugging.

"What's so funny?"

"You are."

"Huh?"

"Farriq, did you really think you could keep Patrice a secret." I didn't say a word when she said that. Shit, what could I say?

"Jari, I was going to tell you about that this morning but you left."

"You damn right I left after the way you spoke to me."

"Jari, I hooked up with Patrice when we broke up. I swear I haven't messed with that chick since we've been back together. You should know that. I haven't been anywhere without you." I could hear sniffling in the background. "Baby, are you crying?"

"Farriq, I could understand the shit happening when we weren't together. You should've told me, but how could you call me when you just left from being with her."

"Who told you that?"

"Check your phone, Farriq." She hung up and a picture

message came through. I couldn't believe there was a photo of Patrice and I coming out the bathroom. If you examined the picture, it looked like she was fixing her clothes. I don't know how that picture was taken, but then I remembered the chick with Rashad that was taking photos of the two of them with us in the background. I called her phone back, and surprisingly, she answered.

"Jari, I can explain."

"Did you fuck her?"

"No Jari, but-"

"But what, Farriq. It's obvious something happened. The picture is worth a thousand words but you're saying you didn't fuck her so what happened?"

"She sucked my dick." I whispered real low hoping she didn't hear me.

"I can't hear you."

"I said she sucked my dick but I didn't let her." I heard the noise letting me know the call ended. She didn't even let me

186

finish telling her before she hung up. I tried to call her back again but she turned her phone off. I know she was at some hotel, because that's where the driver said she was. I hopped in my own car and made my way to where she was. When I got there, they told me what room she was in and gave me a key since I told them I was her husband and gave the man two hundred dollars.

"Why did you hang up on me?" I said scaring her as she walked out the bathroom.

"Get out, Farriq. It's over."

"What's over?"

"Us. This so-called relationship is. It's too much going on for us to be together, and honestly, I'm drained and tired of the bullshit. You slept with some chick when we weren't together, ok, you could've told me. But to go back and let her suck your dick is too much. How would you feel if I told you I met some dude and let him eat my pussy?" I jumped up and pushed her against the wall without hurting her.

"Don't ever say no shit like that again, Jari. No man better not ever touch you."

"I don't want any other man to touch me. That's what you don't get. When we broke up, I didn't run to sleep with another man. I laid in my bed praying every night that you would call or come to me, but you didn't, and now I see why. I cried those entire two weeks because what was supposed to be a joyous occasion turned out to be a nightmare. I walked in on you with your ex, then I found out later who you really were, shot my brother, had my family disown me, and now I'm that same broke bitch I was when my father cut me off."

She moved from under my arm that I originally had blocking her and sat down on the bed. I saw the tears falling down her face, and immediately, I felt like shit. Us being together seemed more like a problem to her, and I didn't want her to feel like that.

"Jari, you know you're not broke. My money is your money. You don't want for anything."

"Is that what you're telling your side chicks?" She scoffed up a laugh.

"I don't have any side chicks."

"Well, your Patrice friend thinks differently. See, she made it her business to tell me about you, her, and the baby in the mall earlier." I ran my hand down my face. This bitch was definitely going to be a problem.

"Funny thing is, she knew who I was and told me how everyone knew my family disowned me and I was a broke bitch. How did she put it? *Your man don't want no broke bitch that sits around the house doing nothing all day.* Farriq, why would you tell her that?" Now she was crying a little harder than before and I really felt like shit.

"Jari, I don't know how she knows who you are. I never discussed you with her and I wouldn't. As far as you being broke, you will never be that as long as I'm alive, and even when I'm dead, my family will make sure you're straight. Baby, you can lay around the house all day doing nothing, and I wouldn't care as long as you have that pussy ready for me, that's all that matters. I don't know how she got that information, but I would never disrespect you like that, especially not to another woman."

"Farriq, why did you let her suck your dick, and is that your baby?" I sat there and told her everything that went on from the moment the shit happened with Tish all the way up to earlier. She listened and didn't say a word.

"Maybe we should take a break. I mean."

"Hell no." I cut her off before she could finish her sentence.

"Jari, I know I messed up today even if it was for thirty seconds, but I won't allow you to walk away from me. That's not up for negotiations. I will go home tonight and give you a couple of days to yourself but that's it."

"But-"

"But nothing, Jari. You and my kids are all I need in my life, and I'm not losing any of you. Baby, I can see how hard it's been for you not working and being away from your brothers. If you want, we can buy a house halfway so you can be close to them. And I know you went to college so if you want to start a business, then go for it. I'll be right there to support you." I told her and kissed her lips.

"I love you, Farriq, but give me a few days."

"You can have all the time you need, but you're still not going anywhere." She laughed and wiped her face.

"This baby has me being such a crybaby. I'm not used to depending on people. I worked for every dime I had, and my father snatched it right from under me."

"Jari, stop worrying about money. I set you up with a bank account, and you know the money has no limit. I would never take it back from you. It's yours, and you can do whatever you want with it except leave me." She laughed and pushed me in the shoulder. "I love you Jari, and I'm going to go so you can get some rest. Call me if you need me. I don't care what time it is." I slid my tongue into her mouth and she happily accepted. I felt myself getting aroused and backed up.

"Be careful driving home."

"I will." I left out her room, went down to the parking lot, and got into my car. I thought I saw someone following me, but once I got on the parkway, no one was there. My phone started ringing and the Bluetooth showed me it was Jari.

"What's wrong?"

"Nothing. I haven't slept without you in months and tonight will be the first time. Can you stay on the phone with me until I fall asleep?"

"Of course. Do you want me to Facetime you?"

"Yea, when you get home." She and I spoke the entire ride back to the house. I kept her on Facetime while I took a shower and got ready for bed. She asked me to plug the charger in my phone so she could stay on while we slept. This woman was spoiled as hell, but I did it care. After she fell asleep, I made sure the phone was on so she could see me if she woke up. Tomorrow, I was taking my ass back to Rashad's house to find out what the fuck was going on.

Chapter 13

Yas

It had only been a few days since we had the family dinner over at Sef's house. Although things with me and Jari weren't perfect, we were in a better place than before, and I felt good knowing that. Sef and I had been waiting to hear back from Rico, telling us the next time we could sit down and meet. The way shit went in the last meeting, we weren't able to fix anything, and we needed to get business rolling again. I wasn't fully recovered, but I was getting around much better now and was driving. At first, a nigga couldn't even shit right, so I was thankful to be up and moving.

The insurance company had notified me, saying that my house would be ready in about a week or so, that was another thing to look forward to. I was enjoying laying up in the hotel with Court, though. I had even upgraded us to a Presidential suite with two bedrooms, and a big ass balcony. It felt good waking up to her pretty ass every morning. Well, except this morning.

When I woke up, Court was still sound asleep but I had to slide out of the warm bed with her so I could shower and start my day. Lying up under her had made me lazy, and I halfway wanted to do business, but today, I had to go to Alia's school for her concert. I'd do anything for my baby girl. If I had to wake up earlier than I wanted to, she had that.

Alia's concert last about an hour. Sef, Rosa, Jari, and myself all attended and was front row cheering our girl on for her mini solo she had. I couldn't help but smile seeing her with her long, curly hair up in a ponytail with a big bow wrapped around it. Rosa had her dressed in a white and pink dress, with some sandals on, and she looked like an angel. Every time I saw my niece as of lately, I couldn't help but think what my child would look like. That had never been a question in my mind, but ever since I met Court, she had me thinking of long-term shit and it was crazy.

After the concert ended, I was on my way back to the hotel, so I could wake up Court and take her out for the day. It was nice out, and I figured that we could take a boat ride or something romantic, or really, we could do whatever it was that she wanted. My phone vibrated, and I saw a text from Chiya. My initial thought was to ignore it, but I guess my curiosity got the best of me, because I found myself opening it.

Chi: Cleaned out my apartment, and I have a box of your things. I'll be here another hour before I give back the keys. Let me know if you're going to come by.

Not even a full minute had passed and another text came through. It was from Court, asking where I was, and as if that wasn't reason enough to take my ass home, I still found myself hopping on the turnpike to head the direction of Chi's house not answering her text.

Chiya opened the door in a pair of Air Max's, booty shorts, and a tank top that showed some of her belly. Her long weave hit her big ass, and she wore some purple lipstick on her lips. My dick rose as soon as she swung the door open and put her small hand on her wide hips. *Damn, she was looking good.*

"What's good Chi?" I asked, letting myself in.

I walked in the living room and took a long, hard look around at all the boxes she had scattered around. It was damn near empty, with the exception of the packed up items.
Chi closed the door, then joined me in the living room and took a seat on the couch.

"Your shit is right there. You can help yourself out." She said, dry as hell.

"Oh word? You hit me with a fake pregnancy and then try to be fake mad with a nigga?"

"Whatever, Yas. Just get your shit and bounce. I got shit to do."

Chi got up from the couch and attempted to walk past me, but I grabbed her by her waist and pushed my body against hers. I don't know why I was tripping off her like this, but seeing her had me wanting to know what her lipstick would look like printed around my dick.

"Yasssss," Chiya half moaned.

I kissed her on her neck, and then, I kissed her on her full lips. Aside from Court, Chi was the only woman I had ever kissed. I had fucked with her for over a year and had grown comfortable doing shit I would never do with everyone. Gripping her by the waist firmly, I lifted Chi up off the ground and wrapped her thick thighs around my waist. We never broke our kiss, as I carried her over to the couch and laid her across it. We both panted in anticipation while I unbuckled my pants springing my dick to life.

"You gonna eat my pussy?" Chi begged, widening her legs.

I shook my head no, placing a condom on my dick. She looked down at it, and she looked offended.

"You better be lucky I'm even giving your lying ass some of this dick. Lift up, Ma. Take these shits off." I damn near ripped her shorts off, tossing them to the side. My phone rang, and I reached down in my pants pocket to pull it out. Court's name flashed across the screen, and I just stared at it watching it ring until it went to voicemail. When she called back for the second time, I looked down at Chi contemplating leaving.

"That's her huh?" Chi opened her legs and dipped two fingers in her wet pussy. I could see her fluids glistening on her fingers, and I could feel my balls start tensing up. Chi had some good ass pussy… I needed some of that shit.

"You know…you want to fuck me, Yas…" she moaned, moving her fingers faster.

Without looking at the screen, I hit end, threw my phone back on the floor then hovered over Chi's body. Her bra was pulled up to her chest, and her big breasts sat up. Sliding a condom on my dick, I cupped one of her breasts, and guided my dick in her middle. I could feel her body stiffen, as she took in all of me.

"Ohh shiiittttt, Yassssss... damn I missed this dick!"

"You missed this dick, huh! Fuck this dick back, Chi. Fuck daddy dick back how I taught you." I groaned, digging deeper into her guts. Chi started lifting her waist fucking me back, as I met her match. Her big breasts bounced around wildly, and I took one in my mouth sucking on her nipple roughly. I could feel her pussy get wetter, and I knew she was about to come for the first time. Chi's pussy always stayed wet... that shit was never dry. That was one of the reasons she stuck around for so long.

"Let... me.... ride it."

I gave two long strokes, before I pulled out of her and sat down on the couch. She climbed on top of me and slid down slowly on my thick shaft. All I could do was hold on, while she bounced crazily on my dick. One hand rubbed on her clit, and she rode me until she came again. After she busted her three nuts, I flipped her over on her stomach and entered her again. Both of my hands palmed her ass cheeks, and I spread them far apart as I stroked her.

"Fuck! Squeeze that shit, Chi!"

"Ohhhhh, babyyyyy! I'm... I'm about to cum!!!"

"Me too! Cum with me, Ma...Arrgggghhhhh shiiitttttt!"

I came so hard I damn near fainted. Using my hands, I held myself up on the couch to catch my breath. Shortly after, I walked into the bathroom to remove the condom then flushed it down the toilet. After I washed my hands and fixed myself, I walked back to the living room where Chi was sitting on the couch with just a bra on. She was looking like she was thinking hard about something, and even though I didn't give a fuck, I ended up asking her what she was thinking about anyway.

"A penny for your thoughts?" I said, as I grabbed my jeans from off the floor and put them on.

"I… I was just thinking… about what happens between you and your little girlfriend now?"

"What chu mean?"

I bent down to tie the laces on my Nikes. My phone was on the floor, and I picked that up before standing. Chi was staring at me with that crazy look again. I was already regretting fucking with her ass.

"What?"

"What do you mean 'what' Yas!" Chi snapped. "I'm asking what the fuck happens now? You came over here fucked me and now-"

"And now I'm about to go home to my girl and take her out on a date." I said. Chi's face was priceless, but I didn't stop and continued to go in. "This wasn't shit Chi, but me needing to bust a nut and you being around at the right time. I still ain't fuckin with you like that, and I'm still fuckin with Court, so don't even set yourself up like that, Ma."

Her face looked like it broke into a million pieces, but I was trying to keep the shit real with her. I really had feelings for Courtney, but I still had my little hoeish ways about me, and I needed to work on and shit. I was sure that I wouldn't fuck Chi ever again, after this time. I guess I just needed to get it out my system or something. Looking down at my phone, I see I had another missed call from Court. I sent her a text asking where she was at and then stuck my phone back in my pocket.

"Look, I gotta go. You straight?" I asked Chi. She looked like she wanted to say some shit, but she didn't.

"Can... can I have a few dollars for gas?" she asked.

"Here." I handed her over five one hundred dollar bills, then gave her a kiss on the cheek. She didn't deserve it for what she did to my crib, but I'd be lying if I said I didn't have a soft spot for her still.

"I'm a bounce Chi. Come lock the door." I said. I made my way out the apartment, forgetting the box I came there for in the first place.

****

The whole ride to the hotel, I started to feel guilty as hell. Never in my twenty-six years had I ever felt guilty for cheating, but right now, I was feeling crazy as hell. I knew if Court ever found out I fucked around on her with Chiya's ass she would stop fuckin with me. I just knew it. My whole ride up the elevator into our hotel suite, I was promising to never fuck around on her again.

The doors of the elevator opened, and I walked into our suite. It was quiet and there was no sign of Court. It was about three in the afternoon, so I didn't know where her ass could be. I tried calling her, but she didn't answer, so I sent her a text asking her where she was. I threw my phone down on the bed and stripped out my clothes so I could shower and get dressed.

When I was finished dressing in my navy blue Nike sweatsuit

and a pair of fresh Nike's, I tied my dreads up, then put on some

cologne.

My phone blinked, and I saw Courtney's name appear

for a text message, telling me she was at the bar in the hood we

called the 43rd. It was a straight up gang banging bar where

mostly Grapes hung at. It was no shocker to me, though,

because that's the type of shit Court was into. She used to fuck

with some Grape OG nigga back in the day before she got

bagged, and the only thing she said about him was he didn't

hold her down like he was supposed to. I was just confused as

to why her ass was chillin over there in her ex-nigga's hood like

she ain't have no nigga. She was tripping. I didn't even bother

texting her back; I just grabbed my keys and made my way to

the hood.

Don't get me wrong, I knew all about Court's past, and I

didn't hold that shit against her, but I wasn't about to be having no chick I dealt with kicking it in the hood with her ex-nigga.

My name was mothafuckin Yassin Abdul; fuck what you heard.

Chapter 14

Courtney

Yas had me all the way fucked up. This morning when I woke up, and he was gone I didn't trip, because Jari had already told me about Alia's concert. I found it funny though, because he was texting me throughout the concert and then suddenly stopped. I was never the type of chick to trip over any nigga, so I wasn't going to even stress the shit being that I'm a street bitch myself. So my last time calling him, I was about to hang up, but he answered the phone, and I heard him fucking that ugly, broke bitch Chi.

I could lie and say I wasn't disappointed, but I was. I knew Yas wasn't perfect, and of course how you get em is how you keep em... but damn, my nigga didn't even wait two months. I sat there and listened for a little bit to confirm that he had fucked that hoe, and then when I got sick of it, I hung up. That shit didn't surprise me though, because I know there's bad in everyone. Being in prison had made me cold and disconnected in a way. It was kind of like, 'And another one bites the dust' for me. No tears were shed, nothing. Just a feeling of Fuck it.

I guess fate had it in for me, because my ex-Weezy hit me up asking me to slide through the hood for some welcome home drinks. I decided to take him up on his offer. I text him back, then got dressed to head to Irvington.

It was a nice spring day, so I chose to wear a white tank top, a pair of stone wash, high-waisted shorts, and a pair of low top, white Converses. My long hair was worn half up in a bun with the back hanging down straight with a blue bandana tied around my head. Gucci frames graced my face, and I wore clear lip-gloss. I was ready to go chill and mack in the hood with my peoples.

Before I pulled up on the block, I stopped by the corner store to grab a water and two pregnancy tests that I could take when I got to a bathroom. My period was late, and I needed to know if I was pregnant before I stopped fucking with Yas' ass. Either way, it was the same damn outcome for me though. I had too much on my plate for kids. I was trying to get my money back and a baby on my hip didn't fit the plans. Especially not Yas' cheating ass. He was a cool person, but we weren't ready for all that.

"What's good Big Court?" Dolla said, as I was walking out the corner store.

"Dolla? What's good nigga?"

"Shit, I see they let a real nigga go."

I laughed and hugged my longtime friend. Dolla and I had grown up together, and when Farriq first put me on, I put him on. The rest was history. He still kept up with me in a few letters over the years and stayed putting some money on my books too. I guess I couldn't complain too much, since he was Weezy's best friend, and even he hadn't done shit my whole bid.

Dolla walked with me down the block to the 43rd bar, where Weezy and his crew were kicking it. A few horns honked along the way with old ass men trying to say hi, and I ignored them all. Dolla started cracking up.

"What?" I asked.

"You… You too fuckin cool you know that."

"Whatever D."

He smiled wide, and I took a second to really look at him. He was so chocolate. Like he was African almost, with the whitest teeth you have ever seen. His light brown eyes were mesmerizing, and he had some deep waves with the most perfect line-up. Dolla was one of those boys who got better looking within their years. He wasn't the dude you and your girls were checking for, but he was the funny one who made you take a double look at him.

"Don't whatever D me." Dolla said. "You know, you really kill me Court."

"How?"

"You...You...You're just beautiful. And it's like you don't even see the shit. Got these clown ass niggas in your face, and they don't even know what they got." My lips parted to speak but nothing came out, and Dolla kept on going.

"Like Weezy? You ain't gotta say it, but I know you still fuck with that nigga. I know if he ever calls you and he in a jam, you gonna come running. And I know that lil nigga you been fucking with got your head all fucked up." I stared at him in amazement. I hadn't even been around Dolla in years, and it was crazy how much he still knew me.

"Wh...who told you?"

Dolla laughed again, and I gave him a little nudge. We were approaching the bar, and there were people standing outside of it smoking.

"Nobody had to tell me nothing Court. I pay attention to you… I know you." For the first time ever, I had looked at Dolla and saw something. I don't know what it was, but it made me feel good. As much as I tried to brush the shit with Yas off, I realized I was more hurt than disappointed.

Weezy stumbled out of the bar with a chick around his arm, and they both looked like they were on some shit. He barely even noticed me as they made their way into his Benz out front. The chick he was with was way past her limit, and aside from the tacky ass dress she wore, her weave was all fucked up. It was funny how, once upon a time, I would have lost my mind over Weezy being with another bitch, but this time, I didn't even feel a thing. Dolla and I stood to the side and watched them drive off without him even noticing me.

"You wanna kick it?" I looked at him and smiled at him. He could always make a situation good, and I loved that about him.

"Yeah, we can kick it. Your moms still live around here?" We started to walk back toward the direction we came from.

"Hell nah. I moved her out the hood a year and some change ago. Follow me to my crib. I'm a pull up next to you." I didn't even realize the Mercedes-Benz truck he hopped in was his until he hit the locks on it and jumped in. My car was parked a little further down the street, I walked to it, got in, and started it up. Dolla pulled up beside me, and I followed behind him making our way to his house. It took a while to get there because he lived down in South Jersey. I noticed we were in Lawrenceville and he pulled into some big house.

****

"Ohhhhh, shiiiiittttttttt," I cried out.

I was nearing my next orgasm, and the way Dolla licked on my clit, I felt like I was about to pass the fuck out. He had been eating my pussy off and on for the last hour and that was in between him fucking the shit out of me. Who knew his dick was this good all these years? I had been overlooking him for sure.

Widening my legs, I pulled his face in deeper so he could tongue fuck my pussy. Dolla was a nasty nigga; he was moaning while eating my goodies, and that turned me on even more. It was like I was cumming back to back just by his touch.

"This...pussy...taste...so fucking good."

"Ohhh, yesssss. Right, thereeeeeee." I cried, grinding my hips upwards. He rubbed his finger against my clit, and I could feel the pressure building up in me.

"Wait-wait-oooohhhhhhhhh,"

"Mmmmmmm," he moaned against my pussy, licking up all the droplets.

Dolla was the mothafuckin pussy monsta for realllll. After cumming so hard the last time, I fell back against his California king bed, and my body was knocked out as soon as my head hit the pillow. I woke up three hours later at almost 11 o'clock, and he was beside me stark naked and knocked out. He was lying on his back with his hands tucked behind his head looking like a model.

Getting out of the bed, I wrapped the sheet around my body and admired his nakedness. He was just the perfect build, with a little bit of hair on his chest that led down to the V-shaped pelvis leading to his manhood. Tattoos covered his upper and lower half, and my godddd his dick was so big. I don't know if it was because I was still fresh home, but that shit did some damage. My phone was going off, and I searched the floor for it until I found it under the bed. It was Yas. *Fuck*!

"He-Hello?"

My breathing was slowing, and I tried to hold my breath in for a while. I was nervous as hell, and I didn't know why, because Yas had already played me the fuck out. Still, I felt like shit.

"Where the fuck you at Courtney!" he barked loudly in the phone.

"Uh...I." I looked over to a sleeping Dolla and went into the bathroom closing the door behind myself.

"I'm at the 43rd Yas." I lied.

Yas damn near growled into the phone, "You at the 43rd? How the fuck is that shit possible when I went there hours ago and you was nowhere to be found! Got me sitting up in there with all them lil gang banging ass niggas! Where the fuck are you at Courtney!"

"I- I left there and went to stop by my friend's house. I'll meet you at the hotel in a minute." I hung up the phone, before giving him a chance to respond. I was leaning against the sink, releasing the breath that it felt like I had been holding. My head was spinning, and I was starting to feel sick to my stomach. My purse was sitting on the counter of the bathroom sink, and I remembered about the pregnancy test I had gotten earlier.

Ripping the box open, I sat on the toilet seat peeing on the side that looked like a brush. I placed the test on the counter, while I wiped and flushed the toilet and began to run myself a shower. The whole time I washed myself in the shower, I couldn't stop thinking about how I had had sex with my friend of years and could possibly be carrying Yas's child. I knew I didn't want a baby, and I knew I didn't want to be with Yas.... But I also knew I couldn't stop fucking with him.

Then, there was Dolla. I wasn't sure if he was willing to just let this be a one-time thing, and I felt fucked up for leading him on.

I washed myself once more, then grabbed a clean towel that was folded on the shelf before stepping out and drying off. After drying completely off, I walked over to the sink and picked up the test on the counter.

PREGNANT.

Fuck! It was literally like my whole world had stopped at that exact moment. Yas calling my phone back again snapped me from my thoughts. I wrapped the test in toilet tissue and stuffed it back inside my purse. When I opened the bathroom door, Dolla was still knocked out. I hurriedly threw my clothes on, leaving my panties off, and got the fuck up out of there. I was going to leave a note for Dolla to call me, but I figured it was best if I made a break for it.

The entire ride to my hotel, I practiced my speech to Yas so we could just end things. He could go his way, and I could go mine, but the moment I entered the suite and saw his worried face, I wanted to shoot him in the face. I kicked my sneakers off by the door and threw my purse on the couch, making my way to the mini kitchen. He was sitting on the couch the whole time watching my every move, but I ignored him. He had some nerve sitting up here with his face all screwed up like he wasn't the one that was fucking. Got me all fucked up.

"So this what hood bitches do? Disappear for hours at a time and lie about where you at?" I ignored him and walked past to go to the bedroom. He hopped off the couch and charged towards me, but I caught him with a right hook to the jaw shocking him.

"What the fuck! Shittt!" Yas yelled, spitting out blood.

"Next time, don't run up on me nigga!"

"You lucky as hell I don't hit women." He said rubbing his jaw. He grabbed my arm. "What the fuck is your problem yo!" I cocked my head to the side, ready to fuck his ass up some more.

"My problem? Nigga, how can you even sit up in my face talking that shit like you didn't fuck that bitch Chiya a few hours ago!" Silence. He didn't say a word. If anything, the nigga backed up giving us some space in between.

"Alright… Courtney, now let me just-"

"Yassin, save that shit. You ain't my nigga no way, and I don't give a fuck what you do in your spare time. Just next

219

time, please don't pick up your phone accidentally when you telling the next bitch to ride your dick like you taught her. I mean, it's the least you could fucking do!" Yas reached for me but I swung again, almost catching him, but I missed. I picked up the thing closest to me and lunged it at him.

"Courtney, what the fuck! You're quick to say we're not together, but you sure as hell acting like we are."

"Get the fuck out, Yas!" I screamed, charging at him again.

He tried to dodge me, but tackled me to the floor. We wrestled for a little, and I tried to get on top of him, but he had my hands restrained above my head. His body rested on top of mine, and he made me face him.

"I'm sorry! Bae… look at me…" he turned my face to look at him. "I fucked up."

"Yea… Yeah you did fuck up, Yassin. You fucked up and lost a real bitch, but it's cool, though, cause I ain't fucking with you like that no more."

His face twisted up, and he just stared at me letting his grip up a little. I pushed him off of me and got up off the floor. He was standing beside me staring like he was about to sneak me so I kept my eyes trained on him.

"So that's what it is?" he finally asked forcibly. "Just like that, you done with a nigga?"

"Yup, just like that nigga." I gave him my back and went to reach for my purse, but he snatched it out my hands. "Yas give me my shit back!"

"Back the fuck up! Your ass wanna disappear for hours and shit coming up in here with your nuts hanging. Where the fuck your phone!" I tried to reach for it again, but he turned around giving me his back rummaging through my purse. My mind went to the positive pregnancy test, and I knew he was going to see it.

I threw a hard punch to his back, "Give me my shit!" I yelled.

He paused stiff, back still turned, and I knew he had seen it. He turned to face me and was holding the wrapped up pregnancy test. My purse dropped to the floor, and there wasn't any sounds or movements for a few seconds.

"You pregnant?" he asked finally. I rolled my eyes at him and walked away.

"What the fuck it look like Yas?"

"So what? You disappear, lie about where you been, and now you pregnant? What the fuck type of shit you off? Court…like…a baby, my nigga? Were you even going to tell me?"

"I didn't disappear any fucking where! YOU were the one who disappeared and lied about where you were. I was where I said I was at, until I left." I spat.

My arms were folded across my chest, and I was shooting him back the same glare he shot me. His light ass was turning red; he was mad as hell, but what the fuck could he really say. He had dipped off too, so who the fuck was he to talk to me about lying and shit.

"Left and went where, Court? Huh?" he asked, moving towards me. "Left to go lay-up with that bitch ass ex of yours?"

"It ain't fun unless the rabbit got the gun now is it!" I swore I saw the devil in him when I said that. He rammed me back into the wall and a sharp pain shot through my whole body.

"Ahhhh, shit!!!" I cried out. Yas wrapped his arms around my neck and stared at me with red, squinted eyes.

"You fucked that nigga while you got my baby in you! Bitch, are you fucking crazy!!!"

"Get…. the…fuck…offffff!" I gasped, clawing at his hands.

"Answer me!!!!" his hands loosened up, but I could feel the pressure still.

"I didn't find out until after!"

"But it was a possibility because you brought the test. Yo, you on some other shit."

I hated the tears that started to fall down my face, because I wasn't a weak ass bitch, but I did the unthinkable and fell for an Abdul, someone who would always have bitches waiting on the sidelines no matter who he was with. Yas looked at me in disgust then shoved me and started to back away.

"Is that even my baby yo?"

"What?" I said in disbelief. "Nigga, the fuck type of bitch you think I am!"

"Obviously, you're the type to fuck another nigga while you pregnant. And let's not act like I didn't hit that shit raw the first night. I didn't even have to ask your name before you had my dick in your stomach."

Wham! I hit him with the remote that I picked up and got in a fighting stance. I swung and my fist almost connected with his face, but he caught me. I started hitting him in the chest again. This time, I kept taking all my frustration out on him, and he stood there taking it. Yas wanted to call me a hoe, but that nigga knows he was the real hoe. Yea, I fucked him the first night, and I was wrong for sleeping with Dolla, especially pregnant with his child, but at the same time, I couldn't feel too bad about what I had done, because he was the one who shitted on me first, and I didn't know. Yas could call me all type of hoes, but he was the real whore and he knew it.

He mushed me in the face hard as hell, and I fell onto the couch. I was so out of breath it took me a minute to get back up. When I saw my keys on the table, I grabbed them and took a dash for the door. I was ready to get the fuck out of dodge because his crazy ass had me acting a fool up in here. With no shoes on, I hauled ass out the door, but was stopped by the sound of a clicking gun.

Click.

"I wish you fucking would step out there. I'll put one right in your head. Try me, Court." I paused instantly and slowly turned back around to face him. "See... we can thump

225

up in this bitch all night, but ain't either of us going anywhere.

You got my baby in you... and ...well; we're going to be a

family. The same way I was raised; in a two-parent home. Ain't

none of that other goofy shit happening here." Yas said, calmly.

This nigga fuckin crazy. I thought to myself watching

him smirking and typing some shit on his phone.

"H-How you going to tell me what I'm going to do with

my body? The only thing you and me need to discuss is your

half of that abortion money. Courtney ain't having no baby

nigga, so if you gonna shoot me then you better trigger up

nigga."

Yas cocked his head to the side and looked at me like I

was crazy. Tucking his gun back by his side, he pulled me back

in the hotel room slamming the door then he turned back to face

me.

"Baby girl.... That's where you got me fucked all the

way up. It may be your body... but that's MY baby. You stuck

with me for life. Ain't either one of us leaving this bitch tonight.

And if we do… well, I guess it will be in a body bag." He turned to walk away but stopped. "Oh, and whatever nigga you were with…. please send my condolences." He left me standing there with my mouth wide open, a baby growing in my belly, and for the first time ever, Fear in my heart.

The remainder of the night, we fought like animals. Well, not fist fighting, more like arguing and yelling. Security had even come up and complained of the noise. Yas cursed them all the way the fuck out. I tried to keep my distance from him and sleep on the couch, but his crazy ass slept right there next to me.

When I woke up the next morning, Yas was in a good ass mood sitting down eating a bowl of cereal. I figured he was in a different space and we could talk amicably about going our separate ways, but all of that went away when he slid me the Sunday paper. The headlines read:

The Trentonian: A man, Donte Harris, age 34, found dead with a gunshot to the head. How the hell did he know who I was with? I felt sick as hell to my stomach.

What the fuck did I get myself into?

I could barely look him in eyes, as I ran off in the direction of the bathroom to throw up. Dolla had been my boy for years; I can't believe Yas would kill him when he had been out cheating on me too. He was so selfish it was unbelievable. After I emptied my stomach contents in the toilet, I hauled ass out of the hotel suite across the hall to where Yajari had been staying. Yas was still seated when I left out, and I was guessing he figured I was going across the hall being I only had a pair of pajamas on. Jari answered on the first knock, and when she saw my face she let me in without asking no questions. She was still staying in a room for whatever happened with her and F.J.

"I swear to God Jari, I'm not fucking with your brother no more. I'm so done with his light bright ugly ass!" I spewed plopping down on her couch. She laughed closing the door

behind me, then followed me and took a seat.

"What he do?"

"What did we do you mean?"

I dropped my head in embarrassment; Jari was mad

cool, and I liked her a lot but the reality was she was Yas' sister.

If I were to tell her that I cheated on her brother, she would

probably pull out a pistol on me. I was always ready for

whatever, but I wasn't really trying to go there with her. I was

pregnant, emotional as hell, and above all things I was in love

with an Abdul. Jari's hand went to my thigh and she offered a

soft smile. I noticed how sun kissed her skin looked, and she

wore her long hair wrapped up in a doobie. A pair of silk

pajamas adorned her body, and her big belly poked out. Hands

down she was beautiful and I could see what FJ saw in her,

probably the same qualities I saw in her bitch ass brother.

"Courtney...I know I was a little rough around the edges

when we first met. I can be a little standoffish at times, and it's something I am trying to work on. But you know like I do, in this lifestyle, you have to watch your back. Everyone is the enemy until proven otherwise… I say that to say, you can trust me. I don't have many female friends…shit I don't have any." We both laughed, because I didn't have any either.

"I want us to be cool. You're family." she said. I nodded my head up and down agreeing with her. Before I knew it, I was sitting there nursing a cup of hot tea and spilling my business to her. It was refreshing talking to another female who understood a lot of the shit I was going through, and I got the feeling she had some things on her chest she wanted to talk about too.

"So after Alia's concert today, Yas and I were supposed to go out. I tried to call him and tell him to bring me a pregnancy test home, because I'm late… but he was too busy fucking that bald headed ex bitch of his. I swear to you Jari, I'm going to kill that bitch when I see her!" I gritted. Jari's eyebrows raised and she looked at me unsure of what to say, but I continued on with my story.

"Anyways, I got mad and I went to my old hood to kick it with my ex-"

"Courtney…"

"I know, I know. I was just so fucking hurt Yajari. And I was angry! I love Yas, I been home what, two months? And he already has my head gone and in the clouds, then the first chance he got to break my heart he did. I didn't know what else to do, I just wanted to take my mind off of things…" I told her taking another sip.

"So like I was saying, Weezy flaked on me and me and my boy Dolla ended up kicking it back at his crib… we…" I pause and glanced over at her. She sat there hanging on my every word too.

"I slept with him." I said. Jari's eyes widened.

"You cheated on Yas? Bitch and your still alive!"

"Barely. Your brother and I been thumping all night girl, I'm surprised you didn't hear that shit." I shook my head.

"Do you know for sure Yas fucked Chiya? I mean you know these little bitches be lying Court-"

"Nah, he fucked her. He accidentally picked the phone up, and I heard the whole thing...Literally." Jari's face showed all the disappointment that I had been feeling myself. Thinking about everything had me hot all over again. My right leg started shaking and I was starting to get trigger-happy. I meant what I said about what I would do if I saw that Chi bitch. It was a wrap for her ass.

"Wow." Jari said.

"I can't even lie, I'm shocked. I mean, I know Yas has always been a womanizer but my brother has been tripping off you heavy since y'all started fucking around. I never seen him act like this with any chick. Not even Chi and they were fucking around for a minute. And what happened with the pregnancy test, are you pregnant?" She asked looking over to me.

My head dropped and I felt a few tears fall. How the fuck did I end up here? A few months ago, I was sitting in my cell imagining all the moves I would make when I touched down. I was supposed to be busting licks and making money, but instead I had gotten caught up with Yas and fell in love. Loving his ass had made me become soft; I wasn't Big Court everyone knew. Instead I was replaced with a fragile brokenhearted woman who I didn't even recognize. Taking my silence for an answer, Jari reached over and hugged me from the side. I could tell the act was strange for her, but she did it anyway and comforted me.

"I don't know what to do Jari," I cried. "Yas and I... It just isn't going to work."

"Maybe you guys just need some time apart." She suggested.

"Sometimes these niggas think that because they love us. We're supposed to just fall in line and take shorts. I know my brother loves you without a shadow of doubt, but I also know Yas is an arrogant ass mothafucka. He's use to women doing what he says and falling at his feet, but see, Courtney you were different. You were a challenge for him. I bet you it was him that forced y'all to be in a relationship wasn't it?" I nodded my head and she laughed.

"See." she said.

"Yas is a different breed boo. He's use to getting whatever it is he wants. And these weak ass bitches like Chi give it to him. Stand your ground, and make his ass work for it. If he loves you, like I think he loves you, he will change."

"And if he doesn't? Jari, I cheated on him… And even though he fucked up too I don't think he will just hold that."

"Then he aint the one for you." she simply said.

"Listen, we all fuck up. I wish there were men out there who were perfect, but then again I need me someone who I can grow with. Y'all will be okay. You'll see. Honestly, I think it may have been a good thing that you bust back at his ass. I'm not saying you weren't wrong, but sometimes these nigga's think just because you have a heart of Gold, there's not a true savage inside. Maybe now his ass will see two can play that game. If he wants to make it work, make him work for it. Just know… no matter what happens between you two, this baby will ALWAYS be good. So don't think about touching my nephew over his ugly ass daddy. Y'all have only been rocking a month or two. That means Yas shot your ass up with his seeds on the first try. That Abdul sperm strong bitch," Jari joked, making us both laugh.

"You gonna be okay girl, watch." She assured me again. "Yas a lil off though, so I wouldn't be too surprised if your little friend was gone by dusk." More tears fell from my eyes, thinking about Dolla. I hated that I had put him in this fucked up predicament where he lost his life behind my shit. He was a good dude and didn't deserve that shit.

When Jari noticed my facial expression she already knew what time it was and pulled me in closer to her. I cried on her shoulder for a few minutes until I gathered myself. A few minutes passed, I wiped my face and decided to change the subject.

"So why you not over at the big fancy house? FJ fucked up too huh?" I said, with a soft smile. My eyes were red and puffy, and I could feel my sinuses started to flare up.
I wiped away my tears and looked at her seriously. Jari's face flushed red.

"I guess Yas aint the only one who doesn't know how to keep their dick inside their pants."

"Farriq cheated?" I asked, in disbelief. Jari nodded her head and rubbed her big belly.

"Yup. Talking about he only let her suck his dick for a few seconds… I swear to you Court, if I weren't pregnant I would have blown that bitch's head off. It's not even his cheating that bothers me, it's the fact that that bitch was the one to send me a picture to my phone. Like where the fuck is the respect? Here I am pregnant with his child, and his cocky ass felt the need to let some hoe suck him off to prove a point?

Fuck him. I got too much other shit I'm dealing with to be worried about Farriq's ass anyway." My mouth was wide open with the tea Jari was spilling. For some reason I thought it was crazy as hell that FJ would cheat on Jari. But then again, Yas hoe ass cheated too.

"Are you okay?"

"Oh, I'm good. I'll be even better when I find that bitch and fuck her ass up. We are going to get the Chi bitch too. I never really liked her stripping ass. Bitch thought she was Sara from Save The Last Dance and shit, talking about she dances. Bitch bye."Jari had me in tears as she sat there going off. What was even more surprising was when she pulled out her phone and pulled up the picture of the chick FJ let give him head.

"Do you know her?" she asked, handing me the phone. I zoomed all the way in to see her face close up. But even then I wasn't able to put a name to the face.

"No...I don't think so. Where is she from?"

"Hell if I know, I just know where her ass gonna end up if she keep fucking with me." I shook my head knowing her ass was dead serious. I could tell being friends with Jari was going to have one of us if not both of us behind bars.

"I know you not going to believe me, but this is really shocking to me. FJ has always been a man with many women, but I've never seen him love anyone the way he loves you. I knew you were different the minute I saw how you were laid up in his house the first day I came by. Trust me… his ass is gone over you. That bitch aint shit to worry about."

"I hear you. I'm sure she's not, just like Chiya isn't shit to worry about. But my name is Yajari Abdul, and I'll die before I let a nigga disrespect me and what I stand for."

Say that shit. For the next couple of hours I kicked it with Jari talking and laughing about anything and everything under the sun. When Yas called her room phone and she told him I was good right before hanging up on him. Although, I was upset, her and FJ were going through some problems.

I was happy she was across the hall because I don't think I would have ever gotten to know her as well as I did. It was crazy how much in common we had with one another. I knew inside my heart, that from this day forward, Jari and I would have a bond like no other.

Chapter 15

Tish

"Fuck that, Rashad. I'm tired of watching both of those motherfuckers live happily ever after." I screamed out to him after he walked away from our conversation. He and I had been discussing bringing down Farriq and the Abdul family. Yea, I was helping for my own selfish reasons, but his reasons were different. Rashad must've wanted the power because he damn sure had money.

"Shut the fuck up, yo! I see why both those niggas didn't have a problem letting you go. Every time I turn around, you're always bitching about one of them. Face it, Tish. You are not wifey material." He started tying his shoes to get ready to go.

"Oh, I'm not wifey material?" I asked and strutted my

naked ass in front of him. I had just stepped out of the shower when we started talking and never got dressed. I stood in front of him and let my towel drop. He looked up and leaned back on the couch.

"Ok, if this is how you want to play. Show me why you're wifey material." He ran his hands up and down my legs as I straddled him on the couch. I felt his man rising through his jeans and couldn't wait to feel him inside. Rashad wasn't working with anything like Farriq or Sef, but he damn sure knew how to make me cum. As the saying goes, it's not always about the size, but the way he can work it, and that's exactly what his ass was doing. My legs were pushed back to my head as he rammed himself in and out. After I came again, I turned around and positioned myself on all fours.

"Fuck, Rashad. I'm about to cum again." I let go and started throwing my ass back to get him to cum. I know it's fucked up to be screwing my baby daddy's best friend, but I was with Rashad first. He and I used to creep before I met

241

Farriq. It's crazy, because they've been friends forever, but because I was never around him, I didn't know who he was. The day I met Farriq was by accident.

"What's up?" I heard a voice behind me say. We were at the club called Providence out in Atlantic City. I had just stepped outside to get some air. It was so damn packed in there, you could barely breathe. Some guy was having a birthday bash and Funk Master Flex was there, which brought everyone out.

"Not much. What's up with you?" He moved in closer, and I could smell him behind me. I'm not sure of the scent he was wearing but it turned me on. I turned around, and he had on Gucci everything. I had to admit that he was fine as hell, and everyone knew who F.J. Coy was. I mean, his name rang bells all through Jersey. Rashad had money, but F.J. was known to have that stupid money. I'm talking the kind you can literally set on fire and not give a fuck because it was plenty more where it came from. I always heard he had a best friend that he rolled with, but I gave zero fucks and was going to do everything in my

power to lock him down.

"Look, I'm not one to chase a woman down, but I've been watching you since you stepped in, and I like what I see. What's up with the two of us stepping off?" He was straight to the point with his approach and I loved it.

"Where are you trying to go?"

"Somewhere to talk unless you have something else in mind." A nigga like F.J. is hard to catch so for him to notice me I had to be careful with my responses. I didn't want to run him off but I also didn't want to rush things just in case he made me his woman.

"I don't know what type of chick you think I am, but if you want to grab something to eat and talk, I'm cool with that. Anything else ain't happening." I wanted to fuck the shit out of him, but like I said, he was known to be a hard one to catch so I had to keep it together. If I threw myself at him like I wanted to, nine times out of ten, he would treat me like a ho and there goes my hopes and dreams down the drain. Hell yea, I wanted him,

but the sex would have to wait.

"Hold up, lil mama. I'm just trying to get to know you."

"Ok then. I just had to let you know I'm not that type of female." *He put a grin on his face, escorted me to my vehicle, then told me to follow him. I sent the chick I was with a message that I was leaving. Luckily, we drove separately, otherwise her ass would have to find a way home, because there was no way I was missing out on this nigga.*

We ended up at IHOP, and the conversation between us flowed naturally. He and I hit it off, and after that night, we became inseparable. We text and spoke on the phone every day, and within two weeks, he made me his girl even before he slept with me. Farriq was definitely a gentleman and didn't pressure me, but after he asked me to be his woman, the very next night I took the dick.

I don't know why I did that, because his ass fucked me to sleep. I swear I got there at six at night, didn't go to bed until after three in the morning, and woke up the next afternoon still tired. He had stamina for days, and I had my work cut out for me.

Over time, he and I started arguing because his father got knocked, and he was handed down the empire. That meant he would be out later, and you already know the bitches were lurking. He never moved me into his home because he claimed that he wanted to build us something for our future family. At the time, I was pregnant so I agreed to keep my place and just stay the night with him. Unfortunately, when Rashad found out we were together, he began to hate me and the feelings were mutual. He would talk shit to me; call me whores and a bunch of other shit. I don't know why when he had a chick and kids.

The day I met Sef, F.J. and I had an argument, and I was coming in the house toting grocery bags. He was outside and offered to help which led me to sucking his dick and becoming his mistress. I didn't know he was married until after I let him fuck me.

"Yo, you got some good pussy and your head game is on point. Let me ask you a question." He said putting his clothes on. I know people call me a hoe, but fuck it, niggas do the same shit.

"What's up?"

"What do you think about being my mistress?" I was shocked because this nigga didn't act like he was married a few minutes ago.

"You're married?" He flashed his ring and smiled. I shook my head because niggas really ain't shit but want to put us down when we do the same thing.

"Yea, but so what? You weren't thinking about if I had someone when you fell to your knees. You down or what?" He asked texting away on his phone. I didn't say anything. He looked up, and I have to say me being a mistress wasn't going to be so bad after all. Shit, in reality, he was going to be my side nigga so why not? Everything was going fine until F.J. found out, left me, got a DNA test for our son then took him away.

Then, Sef's wife found out, and all hell broke loose with that too. Shit, didn't end well for me, therefore, no one should be happy from the way I see it.

Now I'm standing here in the shower once again after I allowed Rashad to fuck me to sleep. I walked him to the door to go, but he turned around, handed me three stacks, and gave me a kiss goodbye. We may not be a couple but he sure treated me like his girl now that his left him.

"A little longer babe and we can take our relationship to the next level." He said on his way out.

"How much longer Rashad?" I started pouting.

"Tish, come on man. Don't do that. You know I hate when you get upset."

"I don't know why. You said I wasn't wifey material; you shouldn't care how I feel." I folded my arms and stared at him.

"Tish, you know I just be fucking with you. You've been down with me since day one and you are going to be my wife. Now take your ass to sleep because I know that's what you're about to do. Call me when you wake up."

We kissed again and he jogged to his car. I shut the door, tossed the money under my mattress, and took my ass to sleep. Normally, I would just leave it on the counter, but with Chiya's broke ass staying here, ain't no telling if she has sticky fingers or not. I was happy as hell she told me she met some white dude at the club she strips at who is willing to put her up in a condo he owns if she allows him to fuck her every now and then. Her ass jumped on that offer and I can't say I blamed her. I woke up to my phone ringing off the hook. I answered it when I saw it was Chiya calling.

"This better be good. I was in a deep ass sleep." I yawned in the phone after I spoke.

"Girl, come in the living room so I can tell you what happened." Yea, we called each other from the other room. I slid my legs to the side and got up slowly. I stretched and walked out my room to the bathroom to handle my hygiene. I may fuck niggas, but a bitch was always clean. I threw some pajama pants and a tank top on after my shower and walked in the living room. Chiya had boxes packed up by the door.

"Damn, you didn't waste any time leaving." I said as she handed me a water from the kitchen.

"Hell no. No offense, sis, but living here is not where I saw myself at. I'm not trying to play you out, because you can't control where you live, but it's not me."

"Trust me, I'm not going to be here much longer either. Once me and my boo finish this shit with Farriq and the Abdul family, we are out." She gave me a weird look but didn't say anything.

"What did you have to tell me?" I put the lid on my water bottle and sat it on the table.

"Oh, so I went to get my things from the old house I stayed at and told Yas to come get his. Anyway, long story short, he and I fucked for damn near two hours. Damn, I miss how good his dick felt inside me."

"Look sis, I'm just going to say this and I won't say anything else." She tilted her head back to drink. "I know you're in love with Yas, but the side chick thing is not a good look. Take it from someone who fell in love with her side nigga."

"Yas, is different though. I was the first person he went down on and-" I cut her ass straight the fuck off.

"Are you stupid? Who the fuck cares if he only ate your pussy? Your shit must not have been that good because he ain't with you now."

"Really, Tish? I know you're not talking."

"I'm not judging you, Chiya. All I'm saying is you two just had a brawl about what you did to his house. Now, he's with Big Court who I can tell you right now don't play no games when it comes to what's hers. I suggest you step away now before she finds out and comes looking for you."

"I'm not worried about her."

"Chiya, listen to what I'm saying. Courtney just came home from jail." I saw her eyes get big when I mentioned that.

"Yea, exactly. That bitch is no joke and even got half these niggas out here scared of her. I know how you feel about him, but do you honestly think he's going to take you back as his girl after what you did to his house? He may have fucked you, but that's all you'll ever be to him. I know I'm the last person who needs to talk, but if I were you I would back up. Plus, when we are finished with them, you don't want to be around that anyway."

"What do you mean when you're done?" I filled her in on what we had going on, even after Rashad told me not to mention it to anyone. But she was my sister.

"I want in." is what she said after I told her. I looked at her and she appeared to be as serious about it as we were. I told her I would let Rashad know and get back to her. If she got Yas to fuck her, she could probably get him to tell her some things that will help us take them niggas down. Fuck it; if I'm not happy, then no one is.

Chapter 16

Farriq

I was on my way to Rashad's house to find out what the hell was going on. The last time I stopped by, somehow that Patrice chick knew I was there, and I lost my girl. Well, I didn't really lose her, but she did say she required space for the time being. The only thing with that was, even with space, we stayed in contact constantly, and if Rashad was really suspect, it might be best for her to stay right where she is. I didn't tell him I was coming by today, so he wouldn't inform Patrice, which now that I think about it, I wonder if it was done on purpose. He and Jari never cared for one another, and I could see him doing that to get me away from her. Rashad was never the type of dude to step in the middle of my relationship. Maybe, it's just because we found out who they really were.

"Who this?" I answered through the Bluetooth in my car. Jari hated that, but she was sleep so I knew it wasn't her.

"This is Miguel, and I'm in town for one night only dealing with some other shit. It would be in your best interest to meet me at the spot. I will only be there for twenty minutes. If you're serious about what we spoke about, you'll make sure you're there." I didn't get to respond, because the nigga hung the phone up. I've always heard he was a rude motherfucker and did things spontaneously. I glanced at the clock, and it was going to take me fifteen minutes to get where he was. I pushed down on the pedal and did eighty the entire way.

The shit between Rico was too much and caused a lot of unnecessary attention, so the best thing right now would be to find another connect. I've heard good things about this dude Miguel, and he was the only person besides Rico that had the purest shit. If I'm going to switch connects, I'm going with the best. I pulled up ten minutes later, because like I said, I didn't want to miss this meeting.

I pulled up to some warehouse, and there were a few black Suburbans and guards standing outside the door. I looked up, and this nigga had snipers on the roof and more guards were on the side of the building. I was checked before I closed the door to my truck and rechecked when I got to the door. I guess he wasn't taken any chances.

"Punctual. I like that." I heard someone say. I couldn't see anyone right away. Some chick walked out, and this had to be the baddest bitch I've seen ever. Her hair hung down her back, and her clothes clung to her body. She wore some red bottom boots and the ring on her finger was shining bright. The sophisticated walk she had proved she had to be a BOSS bitch.

"How are you? My name is Violet. Miguel will be right out." She extended her hand and offered me a seat. I glanced around the room and saw more guards who were staring at me like I stole something. I felt like this nigga was the damn president. The chick walked away, and I refused to look because no man wants another to stare at his woman. I'm not sure if she was his, but she was somebody's.

"You're not a disrespectful nigga either." Someone said, then came from behind the door and walked towards me. This nigga was dressed in normal clothes and a pair of Jordan's.

"Nah. I wouldn't want anyone staring at my woman either." I already knew what he was referring too.

"Good. I would hate to kill you, and we just met. That's my wife, and I don't even want a nigga to say hello if he doesn't have to." He sat down across from me and told me to tell him what I wanted and why I felt the need to change. I informed him that our previous connect wanted us to merge with niggas we didn't rock with, and he agreed that it would make more money, but because of the beef, it would be bad for business. No one wanted to take a step back, and that alone would cause a lot of problems.

"This is what's going to happen." I sat back and listened to him tell me what he expected and what I should expect.

"The delivery drop off will never be the same, and I require the money an hour before. The reason being is that, that will give my people enough time to count it and make sure nothing is counterfeit. It may seem like a short amount of time to figure that out, but I have the best people on my team. If I suspect a problem, you will be cut off immediately with no explanation from me. Oh another thing. I don't do snakes, and as of right now, you have one in your camp." I gave him a crazy look.

"What do you plan on doing about it?" He asked waiting for an answer.

"To be honest, I'm not sure who it is. I've been hearing about my right-hand being the rat, but I don't want to believe it." He ran his hand over his head.

"That's not saying I'm not going to look into it. Now, if what everyone is saying turns out to be true, there won't be a person in this world that will stop me from taking his life. I don't tolerate snakes in my camp nor disrespect."

"That's good to hear, because I feel the same way. I've heard good things about you, and your moms is cool with my aunt. I'm doing this as a favor, because I don't need anyone else on my team." He was cocky as fuck, but I could respect it.

"I'm sure you know who I am, and if anything goes wrong, I won't hesitate to kill you and your family. I'm the type of nigga that will do away with your entire family tree. I don't need any fuck-ups in the future."

"I wouldn't have it any other way." We shook hands and set up a time and place for the first transaction to happen. Honestly, I was happy because that meant that, not only did I have a new connect, but I didn't have to fuck with Rico at all. When I first told him we were parting ways, he tried to say it wasn't happening, but I told him I would never work with the Abdul brothers so he cut me off. Little did he know, my mom was friends with Miguel's aunt, and she put in a good word.

I wasn't going to tell Rashad about the change. Until I knew what was going on, he could stay in the dark. I rode past

Tish's house on my way, and I swore I saw his car leaving from in front of her house; I tossed that shit out my mind. The two of them hated one another.

"I thought you were asleep." I said to Jari when I answered the phone. I hadn't seen her in two days except over the phone.

"I was but my mind was busy. Can you go to the house and call me? I want to see you."

"Ok." I was supposed to be speaking to Rashad, but he wasn't home. I drove to my house and parked my car. I walked up the steps and a smile crept on my face when I opened the door.

"You like what you see?" Jari was lying in the bed naked with her legs open.

"Hell yea. Let me taste that." I took my shirt off, removed all the covers off the bed, and slid in between her legs. I used my two fingers to part her bottom lips and let my tongue slid up and down her slit. Jari arched her back, and the second I touched her, she begged me to stop playing. I missed the hell out of my woman, and I wanted to spend as much time as I could making up for lost time.

"Farriq, make me cum baby." She moaned out, and I swear my dick almost broke through my jeans. She released her juices like a flowing river between her legs that was never ending. I loved licking and slurping all of it up. She overflowed a few more times before I gave her a break. I stood up, undressed and was back in between her legs with the tip at the beginning of her tunnel.

"Fuckkkkk, Jari. This pussy feels better each time I'm in it." I told her watching my dick go in and out. Her cream started turning my man white from the amount of times she let go.

"I love you, Farriq. I never give second chances, and here you are on yours. I swear if you mess up again, it's over. Fuckkkkk, I'm coming again." She moaned, and her entire body began to shake.

"I won't baby. I love you too much to lose you." We

kissed one another hungrily like it was our last time being together.

"Let me get on top." I laid on my back and watched her ride me until I came. We both laid there for a few minutes to catch our breath, then I grabbed her hand and led her to the bathroom to wash up. I couldn't get over the fact that, not only was she having my baby, but she was the enemy I was in love with.

The next day, I woke up and she wasn't in the bed, so I went downstairs; she was in the kitchen making breakfast. All she had on was my white T-shirt that barely covered her ass. I stood behind her, put kisses on her neck, and let my hands roam over her body. Jari's shape was perfect before she got pregnant, and it's even better now that she is. After we ate, we just stayed in the living room lounging around.

"I forgot to give you something last night." She said and crawled over to the couch I was sitting on seductively.

"What's that baby?" I ran my hand through her hair. She

never answered and took me in her mouth. I swear I could never get enough of sexing her.

"Mmmmm, you still taste good Farriq."

"Shitttttt, Jari. I'm going to cum fast if you keep doing that." She was humming on my balls and jerking me at the same time.

"Oh shit, oh shitttttt." I let go and watched her stare at me and jerk my dick until it was soft. I lifted her off the floor and let her straddle my lap.

"You are beautiful, Jari." She smiled and sucked on my neck making my dick hard.

"Make me cum, baby." She was riding the hell out of me. I grabbed her hips and started fucking her back. Her head was back and her titties were bouncing everywhere. I put my hand on her neck and fucked her harder.

"Yes baby, yessssss." We both exploded at the same time. She had her face in my neck as I held her tight.

"Yo Farriq, where you at?" I heard that nigga yell out

behind me. I forgot he had a key to my house. I felt Jari tense up and laid her down on the couch before he came to where we were. I lifted my pajama pants up and told her to put the shirt on.

"Yo, why you coming in my house like that?" Rashad was halfway in the living room by now.

"I have a key, and I always come in here. Why you acting like that?" He said and tried to move past me.

"Nah, bro. My girl in there." I blocked him from going any further.

"Who's your girl?"

"What you mean who's my girl?"

"I'm saying I thought you and the Abdul bitch were over. Is it Patrice?" I shook my head laughing. He kept acting like he wanted to see who it was.

"Rashad, how long have we known one another?"

"Forever why?" He asked following me to the office I had downstairs.

"Then, you should know better than to ever disrespect my woman." I hit him so hard his head hit the floor and he was out. Jari came running in there, and I almost yelled at her.

"Baby, I know you wanted to know what happened and I don't have a problem with that, but I do have one with you not having clothes on and my juices running down your leg. Go get in the shower."

"Ugh, why is he on the floor?" I gave her a look that told her to take her ass upstairs. I sat in my chair and waited for this stupid nigga to get up. A few minutes passed, and he was still lying there. I went to the kitchen, grabbed a glass of water, and threw it in his face. He jumped up and looked around.

"Yo, why did you hit me?"

"Rashad, I don't know what's up with you lately, but I'm seeing a change in you, and it's not for the better."

"Nah, fuck that, F.J., why did you hit me? You'll really put your hands on me over her?"

"If you know why I did it, why would you ask?" I made

my way back to my seat. I wasn't worried about him sneaking me, because he knows I'll put his ass straight to sleep.

"F.J., we have never had any issues until this chick came around, and now you're trying to fight me over her. If anyone has changed, it's you." He said wiping the water off his face with the shirt he wore.

"That is my woman, and you know that. Yea, we had an issue, but no one said we broke up. You come up in here trying to go into a room that I told you she was in. Not only that, you acted like you were trying to see who it was as if I needed to lie."

"Man, come on. You're making this more than what it is."

"Look, Jari is my woman and is about to have my child. You don't have to like her, but you will respect her in my presence and not. I'm not sure what problem you have with her, and frankly I don't give a fuck, but if I chose to be with her, as my boy, you're supposed to support my decision, not try to get me to kill her." I remembered when he first told me who she was and how I needed to kill her. He was right; I should have, but it was too late by then. My heart and feelings were already involved and now no one was going to touch her.

"F.J., you're really going to choose her over me?"

"It's not about choosing Rashad. She has never asked me to do that even after you found out who she was. She has never come out her face and said anything about you and she respected our friendship, but here you are calling her out her name for no reason."

"Fine. If that's who you want, then I'll respect that, but when shit hits the fan, don't say I didn't tell you so."

"Yo, you are one negative motherfucker. What she and I go through is nobody's business but ours." He nodded his head like he understood.

"On to other shit. I cut all ties with Rico and will no longer indulge in the drug game." I wasn't telling him the whole truth, but I did want to see his reaction, and it was just like I thought. A greedy motherfucker will get you caught, and it was a matter of time before he did.

"WHAT???? How are you going to make that decision without me? Where the hell are we supposed to get our shit? This is some fucking bullshit. What happened to you F.J?. Ever since that bitch walked in your life, you've been a different person." My entire facial expression changed when he called her that again.

"Oh, you think I'm playing." I stood up and walked towards him.

"Nah, but if you want a fight over her sneaky ass, then let's do it. Her pussy must be made out of gold." was all he could get out before I hit him with a few rib shots that had him doubled over?

"I told you never disrespect my woman, and you continue to do it like my words don't mean shit. I think it's time I teach you a lesson." I grabbed the gun I had under my desk and hit him on his head over and over with the butt of it. I took

267

out all my frustrations on him and continued until I heard Jari calling my name.

"Baby, it's ok. I think he gets it." I lifted myself up and tried to calm my breaths.

"Yes, Mr. Coy. I think Michael is necessary too. Michael was the personal doctor we had on call. There's a lot of liquid coming out of the spot, and it will need something to cover them." I heard Jari speak in code over the phone to my pops. She took my hand and I stepped over Rashad. We went in the room and she started the shower for me to get in. I had blood all over my clothes and face from beating him.

"I don't know why he hates me so much." She said handing me a towel when I got out.

"Fuck that nigga. You don't have to worry about that. All you need to worry about is my baby in your stomach and keeping me satisfied."

"Oh that's it, huh?"

"Yup. Listen, Jari. I know you're grown and used to

being independent, but I need for you to stay at the hotel."

"What the hell, Farriq? Is there someone else? Why don't you want me around all of a sudden? I'm killing you and that bitch." She turned around to leave, and I snatched her back.

"Calm your little ass down. I want you to stay there, because that nigga will retaliate. I know you can handle yourself, but you're pregnant, and I don't want anything to happen to you or the baby. Can you do that?" She pouted before she agreed.

After the doctor came, my pops sent some guys to take Rashad to his house. I told him I would speak to him tomorrow because I was driving Jari back to the hotel and staying the night. I'm not sure what's going on with Rashad, but the way he was acting showed me something was going on, and I was going to figure it out one way or another.

Chapter 17

Yajari

The shit going on between Farriq and Rashad is worse than I thought. You could tell Farriq was pissed because he called me a bitch more than once, but you could also hear the hatred in Rashad's voice as he spoke to my man. Jealousy and envy are written all over Rashad's face, and I think Farriq was finally starting to see it. I walked into that room and saw an entirely different side of my man. He was beating the hell out of his friend and didn't plan on stopping. I had to yell his name out a few times before he snapped out of whatever zone he was in.

We drove back to my hotel room last night, and I made him turn his phone off and relax. His mom did call my phone this morning to check on him.

"Hey baby. What time is it?" He asked and I glanced over at my phone. I had been up for hours watching shit on Netflix with my earphones in so I wouldn't disturb him.

"It's a little after two in the afternoon." He stretched his arms and stood up.

"Why did you let me sleep so late?"

"You needed that rest."

"You always know what I need. Thanks, baby." He walked in the bathroom, and I heard the shower start. I put the laptop on the bed, stood in the doorway, and watched him get undressed. I had already taken my shower, but I wanted to be next to him. He pulled me in closer and wrapped his arms around my body. We both stood there allowing the water to fall down on us.

"Baby, did you mean what you said about us moving closer and me opening my own business, whatever it may be?" he turned me around to face him.

"I mean every word, Jari. I can't say that I know what it's like to have everything I worked for snatched from under me, but I understand why you feel the way you do. You worked hard for your money and your pops did some grimy shit. I have the bank card with just your name on the card, and you can see for yourself how much money is in the account."

"Farriq, I could've just used the Black Card you gave me."

"I know but there's nothing like your own. Jari, there is nothing in this world I wouldn't do for you and my kids. I need you to understand that." I nodded my head but remained silent. "I'm not the type of nigga that will allow you to struggle whether we're together or not. You can have whatever you want and never use your own money. You won't ever hear how much I do for you come out of my mouth, because it's what you deserve. I told you I loved you, and I meant it."

I wrapped my arms around his neck and kissed him. Instead of sexing each other in the shower, we washed one another up, stepped out, and got dressed.

"What's up Jari?" Farriq asked when he saw my face frown up after looking at the text message.

"Sef just text me to ask for all of us to meet up for dinner."

"Ok, so what's the problem?"

"I don't know if I want to go."

"Cut it out, Jari. You've been to the house already and you made up with your siblings."

"I guess. Are you coming with me?"

"Is that what you want?"

"Of course it is. You guys don't ever have to be friends, and I'm fine with that, but I want you treated with the same respect as I do Rosa and now Courtney. You are going to be in my life regardless, and I want everyone to know that."

"Who said I'm going to be in your life?" He pushed me back on the bed and leaned in placing kisses down my neck.

"I did. Is there a change I need to know about?"

"Not at all baby. I'm not going anywhere and neither are you." After he stopped kissing me, he rubbed my stomach that was now poking out. I was pushing seven and a half months, and I was ready to get the baby out. I felt like something was going to happen soon, and my ass will be too pregnant to help. The rest of the day, he and I went to a realtor's office and started the process of looking at houses. Once Farriq told her there was no limit as far as a price range, her eyes almost popped out her head. She typed some things into her computer, and what do you know? There were a few available to look at today. We still had a few hours before we met up with my family.

The woman had us look at houses in the Colts Neck and Rumson area of New Jersey. The last house we were in, I fell in love with it instantly. There was a total of seven bedrooms with six and a half bathrooms. The master bedroom was huge with a bay window that overlooked the Navesink River. There was a huge kitchen and living room. A fully-furnished basement that Farriq already said was his if we purchased the house. There was also a basketball court and a pool in the backyard. The lawn was huge in both the front and back, and the landscaping on it was beautiful.

"Baby, this is it." He wrapped his arms around me and rested his chin on my shoulder.

"Are you sure?" I turned around with a big grin on my face.

"Yes baby. I love it. Can we get it? Please. Please."

"You know I love seeing you happy, Jari. If you want it, tell her."

"Really?" I was so excited. When I had my other house, my parents picked it. It didn't matter if I liked it or not; they had to make the decision just like everything else in my life. Him giving me free range made me feel like my independence was showing slowly, and I embraced it.

"Yup, but you know I'm making the basement a man cave right?"

"Whatever you want. Thank you so much. I love you." I kissed him and went to tell the woman who had stepped out to give us some privacy that we would take it. Her ass was happy as hell, and I'm sure it was the commission she would receive more than anything. The house was three point five million dollars and worth every penny. He and I finished speaking to the realtor, and she said that, since he was paying in cash, we could move in within the next thirty days. I was happy because the baby would be here not too long after, and I wanted the room to be ready.

"It's that time Jari." Farriq said, reminding me of the dinner we were driving to.

"I know. I'm ok." I took some lip gloss out and pulled the visor down to put it on. We pulled up to some restaurant I never been to, then Farriq shut the car off, and looked at me.

"Are you ok?"

"Yea. I don't know why I'm nervous. I've already broken bread with them at the house. It's something telling me that things are about to hit the fan, but I don't know what. You know that eerie feeling that people get?"

"You'll be fine. I'll be right there." He grabbed my face and placed a gentle kiss on my lips then came around the car to open my door.

"Just think, Jari. In thirty days, you'll be in your new home waiting on the arrival of our son. Soon after, you'll be opening your own business, and I'll be standing right there supporting you." I felt a few tears fall down my face. "Don't cry."

"I can't help it. I didn't think I would ever be independent, and here you are giving me all the tools to do it. I appreciate everything you've done for me, Farriq, and I love you."

"I love you, too, and you don't have to continue thanking me. As your man, I'm supposed to give you whatever you want, and that's what I intend on doing." We gave the waiter our name, and he escorted us to a room that appeared private. The second I stepped foot in that room, I instantly regretted agreeing to come. I turned around, and Farriq looked at me with a confused face. He would, since he hadn't seen anyone in there yet.

"You're late." She said, which caused everyone to look up. I felt Farriq squeeze my hand.

"I'm right here, Jari. I'm not leaving your side." He whispered in my ear, and I nodded my head. I saw the disgusting look both of my parents held and tried my best to ignore them. Yas and Sef both stood up to hug me, and Rosa followed behind with Courtney too. I was shocked to see her there being that she said her and Yas got into it, but if I know my brother, he probably told her she didn't have a choice. Everyone spoke to Farriq except for my parents, and my niece ran straight to him to ask about that damn Pokémon game.

"You're allowing my granddaughter to fraternize with the enemy? I mean, we already see your whoreish sister went and got herself pregnant by him." My mother spoke with such venom in her voice while my dad sat back staring him down.

"Hello to you, too, Mr. and Mrs. Abdul." He spoke to them and my mother rolled her eyes.

"Riq-Riq, I can't find anymore. Can you take me outside to find some?" Farriq glanced at Sef, who nodded his head yes. He knew my niece loved Farriq, and she would have a fit if he didn't let her go.

"Are you going to be ok?" He asked, and then gave Courtney a look and she nodded. I guess he silently told her to keep an eye on me.

"Now that, that motherfucker is gone, let's get down to what we're here for. Youssef, why are we here?" My father spoke to him like he was a child.

"First of all, Pops, calm that shit down." My father raised his eyebrows, and Sef sucked his teeth.

"We are a family, and the shit that happened months ago needs to be discussed so we can move past it and become a family again. I don't know what happened the day we were shot, but dad, how could you take everything away from her like that? I know you were mad, but she worked hard for that money, and she is your daughter."

"Sef, what I do with your sister is none of your fucking business. She went against the family, and that disrespect will not be tolerated." I saw Courtney get up and sit next to me. I guess she could tell I was getting upset from the way I slammed my drink down on the table. The two of them were going back and forth for a few minutes, while my mom stared at me with hatred in her eyes the entire time.

"You know what Sef, just drop it. I have my man, my brothers, Rosa, Courtney, and my niece. I don't need anything from them. I know you wanted us to move past this, but I'm over it. You can at least say you tried." I told him and stood up to leave.

"Sit your disrespectful ass down, bitch." When my mother said that, everyone's head snapped to look at her. "I've sat here and watched you play victim over what happened but never taking responsibility for what you did that started this." I scoffed up a laugh and looked over to Courtney who was shaking her head no. I could no longer be silent. I didn't have it in me.

"You want to talk about responsibility. Ok, let's talk. Do you take responsibility for making me kill all those people over the years? Huh? Or how about the fact that, after I told you that Yas put his hands on me and almost choked me, you didn't agree with me shooting him. How about you and dad yoking me up after you slapped me and dropped me to the floor knowing I was pregnant the day it happened." I saw both of my brothers face change.

"Hold the fuck up. Pops you put your hands on Jari after you tore into my ass for doing it? And Ma, what were you doing slapping her?" Yas asked and neither of them spoke.

"Oh, Brother, that's not the best part."

"Jari, shut the fuck up right now." My dad said standing up.

"Nah, Jari what happened?" Yas said and both him and Sef stood up.

"Your mother said my child was a bastard and-"

"That's because it is. No one will love that child but you."

"Yo, somebody better tell me what the fuck is going on. The level of disrespect is at an all-time high." Sef said moving Rosa away from him. I saw him moving closer to my parents, and Yas was on the opposite side doing the same thing.

"I'm just going to say this, and I'm out. I love all of you, even though you did those things to me Dad and Ma. Your smack could even be forgiven. However, I told you if you came for me or my man, I would come for you. The minute I drop my baby, the war you claimed would be started due to my relationship will happen, but it will be between you two and I."

"Jari, what are you talking about?" Yas said.

"Sef, I forgave you for shooting my man in the back, and Yas I'm sorry for what I did to you, but they are officially on my hit list."

"Hold on, Jari. First off, I didn't shoot your man." I gave him the side eye. "Do you really think I would shoot him while he was holding you. Sis, I knew you were pregnant, and there's no way I would risk harming you or the baby to get at him."

"If you didn't shoot him, then who did."

"Oh shit, that was his boy Rashad. He and I had it out after he did it; that's why he shot me." I turned to look at Courtney, and she was staring at Farriq, who had walked in

283

without me noticing it. The look on his face had me scared, because I knew he was going to kill Rashad now that he heard that. He kneeled down and told my niece he would see her later and told Courtney to make sure I got back to the hotel safe. I tried to run after him but my mother's comments stopped me.

"There you go running after that nigga again during a family discussion."

"A family discussion?" I had to laugh at her. "Ma, why don't you like him? He never did anything to you."

"I don't like him because his mother was a whore."

"WHAT?" We all yelled out at the same time.

"You heard me. His mother is a whore, and his father raised a bastard son, but you can believe that both of their time is coming."

"Ma, tell me you didn't have anything to do with his mother being gunned down in front of him when he was young." I knew she wasn't dead and still had yet to find out what really went down. She smirked, and I tried to lunge at her, but Yas stopped me.

"Let her ass go, Yassin. She thinks she tough; let me show her what a real ass whooping is." My mother said putting her hair up in a ponytail.

"This is what it has come to huh?" I asked her.

"What did you think, Jari? That you would bring him with you, and we would sing Kumbaya. I mean, come on; he's is the enemy." My father said staring at me.

"Rosa, take my daughter to the car." Rosa looked at Sef. "NOW!" he screamed out, and she hauled ass out the restaurant.

"Ma, I'm not going to fight you, because I'm with child, but you can bet when I deliver, these hands will be waiting for you. You want to treat me like a bitch off the street, then I'll forget who you are and do the same. And dad, you're sitting there silent, but what you did won't go unnoticed."

"Shut the fuck up, Jari."

"Why do you want her to shut up, Pops? You've said that to her twice already." Yas and Sef both stood there waiting on his answer.

"Oh, he doesn't want either of you to know that, when the both of you were laid up after he and your mother put their hands on me, they tried to have me killed. Twice, I may add, but you know your sister handled herself." Courtney covered her mouth.

"Courtney, get her out of here." Yas said to her, and I felt her trying to move me.

"I never thought my own parents would try and kill their own daughter, but I guess neither of you give a fuck about anyone but yourselves." Not even thirty seconds later, Sef had hit my father so hard he knocked him out.

"Sef, did you really just hit your father?" My mother yelled out running to his side.

"Ma, I don't know what the hell happened to you, but stay away from me, my brother, Jari, and my family. I can't have the two of you bringing that bullshit to my house. Let's go, Jari. I stared at Yas, who was giving my mother the death stare. He was a momma's boy, so I know all of this had to be doing something to him.

"Hello, Zora." All of us turned around, and there stood Farriq's parents.

"What the fuck? How in the hell are you alive, and you? How are you out of jail?" My mother yelled out. The fear on her face was evident, and if I was thinking clearly, I would've taken a picture.

Chapter 18

Rashad

"What the hell happened to you?" Tish asked when she opened the door. I pushed past her and noticed the chick she called her sister lying on the couch. She jumped up when she saw me sit on the opposite couch. I stared at her to see if I knew her from somewhere but I didn't.

"Me and that nigga Farriq finally had it out over that bitch he's with." I wasn't going to tell her he whooped my ass. For all she knows, I did that to him.

"What? When? Why?" Tish asked, shutting the door and copping a squat next to me.

"I stopped by there, and this nigga had some bitch laid up in the living room. I'm guessing they just finished fucking because he blocked me from going in there like she was naked. Then I called her a bitch and his ass got mad." I saw Tish cover her mouth as if I said something wrong.

"Come on, Rashad. You know as well as I do that he doesn't play when it comes to his woman or his kids. You were the same way about your ex so why would you go over there and say that?"

"Fuck that bitch yo. Ever since she came in his life, it's been nothing but problems. I swear I can't wait until Patrice finally takes those motherfuckers down."

"Wait. Didn't you say she was pregnant by Farriq? Do you really think she'll go through with it?"

"That bitch better if she knows what's good for her. I paid her a lot of money and we're almost at the finish line. It's too late to turn back now." I told her. I stood up, grabbed her hand, and had her walk to the back with me. My ass was horny as hell and the chick on the couch didn't make shit any better by the way she stared a nigga down. When she got up and her ass hung out the bottom of those pajama shorts, I had to adjust myself without Tish seeing me. This was supposed to be her sister, but I could already tell she wasn't shit.

"Suck that shit, Tish." I moaned out as she gave me head. I opened my eyes to look down at her and her sister was standing at the door playing with herself. I put my hand on the back of Tish's head to make sure she didn't turn around and see her.

"Hell yea, girl. Just like that." I said making Tish think I was speaking to her. The girl had her leg up with her fingers inside. I saw her juices seeping out, and her body started shaking. After I saw she was finished, I lifted Tish up and sat her down on my dick with thoughts of her sister being the one riding me. I know I wasn't shit but fuck it. After an hour of us getting it in, Tish and I took a shower and she was down for the count as always.

I was lying there with my hands behind my head in deep thought hoping Farriq was brought down. I felt a tap on my shoulder, and I looked up to see her sister standing over me naked as the day she was born. My dick sprung to life instantly. I moved out the bed and followed her to the other bedroom and locked the door.

"I need to feel you." She whispered and pulled me closer to the bed.

"You got that, Ma. Make it wet for me." I stood over her and watched her play with herself while I stroked my dick. She was about to cum, so she stopped to take my man and place him at her entrance. Thirty seconds later, I had shorty bent over, ass up and face in the pillow screaming. Luckily, they were muffled because Tish damn sure would've heard her. She and I fucked as quietly as possible in that room. After we had finished, I gave her my phone number, hit her up with some cash, and told her I would definitely be returning to dig in those guts. Her pussy was way better than her sister's. I eased back in the bed once I showered again and pulled Tish in close to me. I did love her, but I was still a nigga, and if a bitch offered, I took it. I was just getting into my sleep when I felt something cold against my head.

"You're about to die motherfucker." I heard Farriq say as he cocked the gun back. I should've been in fear for my life, instead I was staring at the person standing behind him doing the exact same thing.

"Nah, Farriq. I think it's going to be the other way around."

To Be Continued...

Text Shan to 22828 to stay up to date with new releases, sneak peeks, contest, and more...
Check your spam if you don't receive an email thanking you for signing up.

Text SPROMANCE to 22828 to stay up to date on new releases, plus get information on contest, sneak peeks, and more!

CPSIA information can be obtained
at www.ICGtesting.com
Printed in the USA
LVHW04s1523170918
590425LV00012B/1054/P